GATHERED DUST
AND OTHERS

W. H. Pugmire

DARK REGIONS PRESS
– 2018 –

DEDICATION:

This book is dedicated,
with fondest love, to

JEFFREY THOMAS.

Contents

The Strange Case of Wilum Hopfrog Pugmire

An Introduction by Jeffrey Thomas

-1: In Search of the Author-

I am thrice honored to have the opportunity to write an introduction for highly regarded weird literature author W. H. Pugmire, and so I realized I would be a bit challenged in regard to what I might say this time that I haven't covered before. Not that I am ever at a loss in my enthusiasm for Pugmire's fiction, and the collection you hold in your hands is to my mind of particular merit, displaying as it does the breadth of Pugmire's skills. Herein you will find work set in his infamous Sesqua Valley in the Pacific Northwest, but the settings are by no means limited to that location. Furthermore, there are prose poems in addition to story. There are lengthy works but also the very brief (but no less powerful!) vignettes that were my first exposure to his writing. No, the challenge I would face when composing this introduction would be of another kind, the nature of which I could not have foreseen.

A few years ago at my blog I posted an interview with Pugmire that went over quite well, so my first thought was to invite the author to do a new and updated interview here as the real focus of this introduction. To that end, I sent an email to the author. And another. And another. I realized he might be preoccupied; to complete this book, which I also edited, he had immersed himself in a frenzy of creativity that had consequently required him to set aside other projects of his in the works. Surely he must be busy now with resuming those neglected projects. But as the days went by, and more emails and even an attempt to reach him by phone elicited no response, I admit that I grew a bit anxious (dare I admit, impatient?) about completing my introduction so that I might be free to return to projects of my own that I had been forced to set aside while editing this collection. And so, I thought, why not simply reuse the interview I'd posted at my blog, since it had never been in print? What follows then is the bulk of that interview…but what follows the interview is more of my confusion and anxiousness regarding the strange disappearance of Wilum Hopfrog Pugmire.

-2: The February 26, 2009 Interview-

W. H. Pugmire is an irony, a paradox, one of my very favorite writers. Why? Well, he plainly identifies himself as a Lovecraftian author, and writes stories that often link directly to the Cthulhu Mythos, and yet he is also one of the most unique fantasists I have ever read. His work, his voice, is distinctly his own. Where Thomas Ligotti's brilliant dark stories creep one out for being so bleakly sterile, so lacking in a sense of humanity, Wilum's work is quite the opposite – seething with tormented, but also exultant, emotion. His stories are often about outsiders finding either ghastly doom or cosmic communion (depending on how accepting they are of the fantastical events that are presented to them), with a recurring theme of transformation. His style is richly poetic. Here's an excerpt from his story THE MILLION-SHADOWED ONE (which, incidentally, Wilum wrote for my son Colin when he was discovered at age four to be autistic):

"The small creature hobbled close, and I took in the weird shape of its head, the cloudy and colorless eyes, and mutation of its ungodly form. It took my hand and brought it to its wide nostrils. Smiling, it shut its awful eyes, began to shudder, and I felt my blood grow cold as its fleshy form began to blur, to grow momentarily indistinct. And my hand, the hand it held, faded as well, and with that invisible hand I seemed to touch another realm, a place beyond the rim of time and space."

This excerpt demonstrates so many of Wilum's skills. Eerie imagery, striking imagination, poetic prose, a sense of the cosmic and a melancholy poignancy, all in one brief passage. That pretty much says it all about Pugmire. Or does it? I decided to let him do the telling, himself, in the following little interview:

* * *

JET: Wilum, most of your work takes place in your own milieu of Sesqua Valley, in the Pacific Northwest. How, why, and when did this setting occur to you?

WHP: It was around 1974, when I decided to become a famous Cthulhu Mythos writer just like my heroes Brian Lumley and August Derleth. When young Ramsey Campbell first began to write Mythos fiction, which he sent to Derleth, Ramsey set his tales in HPL's Arkham, Dunwich, &c — and Derleth wisely told him to invent his own setting, based on a place he knew. I instantly wanted to base my milieu on North Bend and the Snoqualmie Valley. It had to have a "qua" sound to it, like so many towns here in the Northwest, so I came up with Sesqua. North Bend's hypnotic Mount Si became my Mount Selta. Later, the area was used for TWIN PEAKS.

JET: The silver-eyed natives of Sesqua Valley are very attuned to the magic of their valley, as opposed to many Lovecraft characters who are only destroyed by their encounters with the fantastic. And your work contains a lot of supernatural elements, where Lovecraft's did not. What else do you think differentiates your work from HPL's, and where do you think your work aligns with his?

WHP: The reason I write weird fiction is to pay tribute to H. P. Lovecraft — that was how I began, and that need to pay tribute is still keen within me. I am an OBSESSED LOVECRAFTIAN and hope to remain so forever. When I began writing I was a clueless Cthulhu kid, indoctrinated by Derleth's TALES OF THE CTHULHU MYTHOS and Lin Carter's A LOOK BEHIND THE CTHULHU MYTHOS. From those gents I "learned" that the way to pay tribute to HPL was to invent your own Old One monster and your own Dark Book — all of the stupid clichés. As I matured, I sensed that I needed to "return to Lovecraft" and let his fiction alone inspire my Mythos work. But my imagination isn't cosmic — it's supernatural. Where my fiction aligns with HPL's is in my obsession to write Literature, to create literary art, to write beautifully. In themes, we are very different. My fiction is emotional, his is intellectual. Most of his characters flee from the horrors; mine ARE the horrors, or long to be so. But this, too, I learned from Lovecraft, from the endings of "The Outsider" and "The Shadow Over Innsmouth," where the narrators embrace that which makes them Outsiders.

JET: In recent years I've noticed that you have used recurring characters in your Sesqua Valley stories, such as Nelson, the goat-faced sculptress Edith, the canine-faced poet Richard Lund, Adam Webster, the Whateley siblings, and most notably Sesqua's "firstborn," Simon Gregory Williams. What inspired you to do this?

WHP: In writing about the small town of Sesqua Valley, I had to portray its inhabitants. I love recurring characters like Randolph Carter and Titus Crow. So I just naturally had characters return from story to story. Once in a while I had to create a new one, to help move the series along. My most popular character, and my personal favorite, is Simon Gregory Williams. He's such a bad-ass freak.

JET: You've also been expanding on and revising earlier work, and writing longer fiction than you once did. How did this come about, and how do you think it's working out for you?

WHP: Stanley Sargent (*another talented writer of the Mythos – ed.*). He kept daring me to try and write a novelette. I never thought I could. I knew I wanted to grow and mature as a writer, and one way of maturing was to write longer tales. So I began to experiment. After coming home from my first Lovecraft Film Festival, I had to complete THE FUNGAL STAIN. I told myself, "Okay, I'm gonna write a story and it's gonna be FIFTY PAGES!" Instead of writing that story in longhand, the only way I used to compose, I typed the rough on the typer, so that I knew it would come to fifty typed pages. And when I completed that polish of "Your Metamorphic Moan," it was fifty pages exactly! And now it's much easier to write stories of length. My finest story is the one I wrote for Joshi's BLACK WINGS anthology, "Inhabitants of Wraithwood." It is also my longest tale, over 13,000 words. Now, I approach story ideas in a different way, as a mature artist with new-honed skills. But my core inspiration remains the same — to pay fictive tribute to Lovecraft.

JET: Besides Lovecraft, who are some of your favorite authors?

WHP: I don't read modern horror. My one modern book addiction is biographies of writers, painters, poets, bohemians — those I DEVOUR! My favorite authors are Oscar Wilde, Henry James,

William Shakespeare, Thomas Ligotti, Franz Kafka. I have a passion for poetry. I recently got the Penguin collections of Maugham's short stories, and I'm enjoying those. I need Literature with a capital L. I need works that nourish my mind and soul, that instill within me that burning ache to join the club and write, write, write!

JET: What is your work routine like? Do you write in the day, in the night? For long or short stretches? Do you listen to music while you write, and do you drink your favorite orange cappuccino during this time?

WHP: Oh my gawd! — orange cappuccino was such a drug, as you well recall. Now it's too harsh, I cannot drink it! Real coffee gives me heartburn. When I returned to Mormonism, I tried to give up all forms of coffee, but that proved as impossible as giving up Dior lipstick. Now I drink General Foods decaf French Vanilla — it's my fake coffee heaven. I have no routine because I lack all discipline, alas. Since going online I am now accessible to publishers and I'm getting more and more offers. So I need to write full-time. I moved in with my mom, who is crippled with age and can no longer live alone; and I have some friends who are supporting me as Patrons — so deliciously Victorian! I try to write whenever I can. If the weather is good and mom wants to do yard work, then my writing day is pretty much shot. I spend a lot of time sitting here before my keyboard TRYING to write. Or I'll sit here and read Wilde, Poe and Lovecraft and make notes which bloom into inspiration for stories. I need absolute silence when I'm writing, can't listen to Barbra or Boy George — although I've tried, but then two hours have gone by with me sitting here singing "People" and "Do You Really Want To Hurt Me?" but with nothing on my laptop screen. When it does begin to flow — and that is when I am the happiest girl on earth — then I write very very quickly. Zoom! I now write all roughs right on ye laptop, then I go and polish, restructure, rewrite entire pages. I'll print out a page that seems okay and read it aloud, and then do some more polish on it. The important thing, for me, is to always be here, sitting at the keyboard, trying to write, or pretending that I'm trying to write. Sooner or later, it begins to flow.

JET: How did you become attracted to writing? And why weird literature?

WHP: I've always written. As a gay boy I wrote my own Broadway musicals, book, lyrics and music. As a young Mormon I wrote skits and little plays for the church. When I discovered FAMOUS MONSTERS OF FILMLAND I began to do my horror film fanzines, and for the one I did in college I had Robert Bloch write a tribute to Forry Ackerman. When the church sent me to Ireland as a Mormon Missionary, they wouldn't let me watch horror films — too evil. I was corresponding with Bloch, so I began to buy his books, and also anthologies that had his stories in them. I got hooked on weird fiction, had to buy a wee suitcase just for all of the British horror paperbacks I was collecting. When I love something, I need to express that love with writing. So I began to write horror fiction. Came home and discovered Arkham House and became a Cthulhu nut. The more I studied Lovecraft's fiction and read his letters, and the more I read S. T. Joshi's LOVECRAFT STUDIES, the more I wanted to write mature, artistic Lovecraftian fiction. I'm now just beginning to do so.

JET: Could you provide us with a little more background, if you would?

WHP: Tell my sad little life story? I was a weird kid. Believed I was a Witch when very young, as did my older sister. She and I used to practice what we thought was magick. Grew up knowing I was a sissy (loved playing house with the neighborhood girls, but always dressed LIKE them, wearing play dresses &c) and being tormented for it by grown-ups, kids at school, and thus I became an introvert and created my own realms of reality where I could be safe. My best friend in high school was Jewish, and that began a Jewish identification. Later I learned that I AM Jewish on my mom's side of the family. Fell in love with Streisand while in high school, where I was heavy into drama and was certain that I wanted to be a professional actor. Did theatre for a while when I returned from my mission, but more and more I wanted to be a Mythos writer professionally. Began to visit with Harold Munn, who as a young man used to hang out with Lovecraft, driving HPL around sightseeing in New England. Came out as queer and everyone freaked out, got kicked out of the church, kicked out of home. Dropped out of the Lovecraft scene and everything and moved in with my granny. Discovered punk rock, and it saved my soul. Did my famous fanzine, PUNK LUST. Returned to writing and sent "Pale,

Trembling Youth" to Jessica Salmonson for her FANTASY & TERROR magazine. She added a new beginning to it and sold it to CUTTING EDGE. Returned to writing full-time around 1985, the same time I discovered how much fun it was to walk around Seattle dressed like Boy George, blending drag with punk, safety pins and mini-skirts. Some Mormon missionaries knocked on my door some seven years ago. I told them ain't no way I'm returning to Mormonism. They said try praying about it. Alone, I got on my knees and had such a violent, overwhelming, shocking experience, felt my dead father and grandfather in the room with me, shaking, weeping, howling, telling God, "Don't do this, I don't want to change my life!" But I learned beyond personal doubt that God lives and that he's a Mormon, so I returned to the church, which has made life extremely interesting, difficult, absurd, wonderful.

JET: You only recently went online, with email, joining message board conversations, and so on. Why now, and how are you liking it?

WHP: I said Never Never Never. Beginning with THE FUNGAL STAIN, S. T. Joshi became my "official" editor. When Jerad Walters of Centipede Press said he wanted to publish an omnibus of my best weird fiction, S. T. hinted that it was time I get email so that I can send him my work electronically instead of sending him typed MSS that needed to be scanned. My patron hooked me up, and I'm totally fucking addicted. Such a cliché. I LOVE meeting Lovecraftians online, talking about Cthulhu Mythos, &c. …

-3: Broken Off-

From here, the interview went on to list books that Pugmire had already seen released or was anticipating. While the information related in the interview to this point is general and remains pertinent, the information that follows might now be dated: incomplete or inaccurate. One book's title was changed, book contents were altered, projects in the works have been completed and more added. A more up-to-date bibliography of Pugmire's work to the *present day*, taken from the author's Wikipedia page, would now read:

TALES OF SESQUA VALLEY, 1997, a chapbook

released from my own Necropolitan Press, similarly with an introduction by yours truly.

DREAMS OF LOVECRAFTIAN HORROR, 1999, Mythos Books.

SONGS OF SESQUA VALLEY, 2000, a chapbook from Imelod Publications.

TALES OF LOVE AND DEATH, 2001, a chapbook from Delirium Books.

A CLICKING IN THE SHADOWS AND OTHER TALES, 2002, a split release with Chad Hensley from Undaunted Press.

SESQUA VALLEY AND OTHER HAUNTS, 2003, a hardcover from Delirium Books.

THE FUNGAL STAIN AND OTHER DREAMS, 2005, Hippocampus Press.

SESQUA VALLEY AND OTHER HAUNTS, 2008, a revised edition of the 2003 release with three additional stories, from Mythos Books.

WEIRD INHABITANTS OF SESQUA VALLEY, 2009, Terradan Works, with another introduction (and cover art) by yours truly.

THE TANGLED MUSE, 2010, a massive omnibus from Centipede Press.

With SOME UNKNOWN GULF OF NIGHT, Arcane Wisdom Press, due in 2011.

In any case, I now had the meat of an introduction, but that didn't answer the question of why my longest-running and closest writer friend was now not responding to my messages, when throughout the editing of his book we had been in constant contact. Had I inadvertently offended him, alienated him somehow? It hardly seemed like Wilum to hold a grudge, so curious as to whether this silence had to do with me alone, I checked his frequently updated page at the social networking website, Facebook, only to find he had no longer been frequently updating it. For more than a week, he had not written what is called a status update, and several friends had posted on his "wall" asking about his whereabouts before me. His last status update had been exceedingly brief and cryptic, and maybe it was just my own overactive imagination that imparted inflections of bewilderment, awe, perhaps even terror into its single typed word: *"Night-gaunts?"*

-4: The Video-

I decided to check another venue where Pugmire has created a presence for himself; the video-sharing website YouTube, at which, as "MrWilum," he has posted many "vlog" entries – a vlog being a video blog. Here, he has discussed his current projects, and the works of other authors he admires such as, of course, H. P. Lovecraft.

But again, I was to find that the most recent video Pugmire posted was over a week old. Videos up to that point had discussed his work on this very book, with titles such as: *W. H. Pugmire reads from his work in progress*; *'Depths of Dreams and Madness' – a reading*; and the second-to-last last video posted: *A Weary, Rambling Vlog*. But even that video, with its perhaps significant title, turned out to contain nothing more alarming than Pugmire – as always, speaking intimately to his webcam in the basement of his mother's place, with a mundane wall hanging of two extinct Kennedy brothers peering over his shoulder – again discussing his work on the collection GATHERED DUST AND OTHERS. No, it was only the most recent vlog entry uploaded to the site that caused me concern.

The video, which was untitled, showed nothing much more than a field of shifting static, like a sandstorm of volcanic grit raging just beyond a thin glass windowpane. I persisted and stared at this video throughout its full fifteen minutes, however, and gradually I could just make out a head and shoulders somewhere behind all that static, darker as the vague figure apparently leaned in closer to the camera -- but then it would fade entirely from view again, before once more briefly surfacing. I had never before known Pugmire to use any special effects such as my own webcam possesses to make his videos look bizarre, but that isn't to say he might not experiment thus.

Even so, wouldn't he at least want his viewers to hear his voice? And yet the sound accompanying the blizzard of pixels was also just a sizzling, hissing barrage of static. Only when the vague figure almost became a familiar outline did I hear half-drowned, greatly distant snatches of words. I believe I heard: "*Sesqua Valley...I made it feel* (or, *I made it real?*)...*she wants her mask back...seven worlds...Gershom! This is Gershom!*"

The only other thing I discerned occurred at 14:52 in the video, just before it ended. In a corner of the video window, I caught a brief glimpse of several faces. Surely, those portraits of John and Robert Kennedy on the wall hanging behind Pugmire, as always. But when I played the video back and paused it at 14:52, freezing those obscure visages, they proved to be something else. Something not quite human – gazing back at me with mouths open far too wide in hunger.

No...no...again, surely this was a product of my own writer's imagination.

I can only – *I must!* – assume that Pugmire erred somehow in uploading this video, or that the video itself was corrupted, unbeknownst to him. I can only hope that he will delete this disturbing fifteen minutes soon, and in its place leave one of his more familiar videos, in which his soft voice reads enthusiastically from whatever wonderful new piece of work he is bending his talents to.

Though I cannot wait until then to complete this introduction and submit it to my publisher, I will check back constantly for that next video to appear. Hoping, yes, hoping that it will show more clearly Pugmire's own face next time, and not reveal more clearly, instead, those other faces I believe I glimpsed floating hungrily in the raw stuff of unknown dimensions.

-- Jeffrey Thomas, Massachusetts, 4/25/11

Gathered Dust

(Dedicated to ye memory of J. Vernon Shea)

I.

I never solved the mystery of how my Uncle Silas came to own Elmer Harrod's haunted house in Arkham, but I suspect it had something to do with his fondness for campy horror films. Harrod owned an impressive collection of such cinematic silliness, which filled the area that had been turned into a tiny movie house where he invited guests to view his favorite films as well as his own home movies that had been filmed in the nearby cemetery. These homemade efforts served as Harrod's introductions to horror films on the television program where he served as horror host, and I used to love watching them when, as a teenager, I would spend two weeks of every summer with my uncle; and I recall how something caught my attention, an expression reflected in Elmer Harrod's shadowed eyes, momentary hints of authentic mental disturbance and bewilderment and subtle fear. Harrod's local fame as weekend host to televised horror films was matched by the legend of his haunted house, a mammoth Victorian pile that had been the subject of nameless rumors for decades in Arkham. Harrod was less renowned for the paperback anthologies of weird fiction that he had edited over the years, short-lived titles with lurid covers; nor was his one novel, *Underneath Witch-Town*, what could be called a success, although I had found it an enthralling read after having found a box of copies after my uncle had purchased the residence and its contents. It was the library of the place that really influenced me, however, for it was stuffed with the horror host's extensive collection of weird phantasy. I spent summer after summer poring over those books, and it was under the spell of their authors that I became determined to join their ranks and write horror fiction professionally. It was while stumbling through the high grass of Old Dethshill Cemetery that I came up with my pen name, Deth Carter Hill. There were many Carters buried in the forsaken place, but I had been peculiarly drawn to the hidden grave of Obediah Carter, whose tabletop tomb dated 1793 to 1887 was decorated with a faded photograph of the elderly gentleman beneath an oval of glass that has been fastened to the slab of stone. There had long been legends that the Carters of Arkham had been tainted with witch blood, and one could well believe it when examining the stern and satanic countenance of Obediah Carter as it peered from its aged photograph.

I came to inherit the queer Victorian residence after my uncle's insane suicide, and I happily made the move from my cramped apartment to the spacious abode, where I was surrounded by elements of ghastly horror collected from various pockets of the globe by the two previous owners, things that I knew would aid my career as a weaver of weird tales. It did not deter me to bask in the notoriety that came my way, to the aid of my creative reputation, by the scandal that arose from my uncle's incomprehensible self-extinction. The papers had been full of it for a little while, of how my uncle's corpse had been discovered hanging from a strong length of vine attached to a hideous tree in Old Dethshill Cemetery, and of how the end of the vine that had tightened around his broken neck had implanted itself into the flesh of Uncle's ravished throat.

I found, during my first two months of residence in Arkham, that Uncle Silas had gained a curious reputation in the town, for it was whispered that he never ate, was never known to shop for groceries or dine out; and the fact that he was often seen haunting the abandoned cemetery at night gave way to gossip of vampirism and other such nonsense. It was when I discovered my relation's own home movies that I learned how uncanny truth can eclipse the wildness of paltry rumor; for Uncle Silas had followed Elmer Harrod in the practice of being filmed within the wild confines of the haunted burying ground; but where the horror host had brought in a film crew to record his outlandish behavior among the tombs, it seemed that my uncle's was a one-madman's crude operation. On one spool of film he had recorded himself dancing among the rotting stone slabs and speaking the most outlandish gibberish I have ever heard, in what must have been a language of his own invention. He seemed almost to chew his lips as he drooled and muttered a name I could not quite make out. I found a film that showed him reclined on the slab beneath which Obediah Carter slept, and the dim electric light that he had somehow been able to set up caught to perfection the weirdness of his facial distortions, with which he mimicked the actual visage of the dead sorcerer. The most disturbing images that I found, however, were caught on the three rolls of film that showed my old relation twitching before the unwholesome tree on which he had ended his life. On one spool of celluloid he is shown wrapping the tree's weird pale vines around his arms and ankles and then pirouetting like some deranged puppet; and it was so disturbing to see how the withered old tree, in the uncanny light of my uncle's source of illumination, took on the imagined semblance of a gigantic bestial claw that curled its grotesque distended digits in night air.

My uncle's experiments with filming seemed to incorporate some kind of trick photography near the end, for on the last spool of film he is shown in close up, dangling from the vines of the tree, vines that resembled cloudy veins through which a dark substance flowed in the direction of my uncle's upraised arms, into which the vines had penetrated. Uncle Silas did not regard the camera as he muttered, "More, more – my arms are hungry." I watched all of these films with a sense of growing horror, and then I stored them away and tried to forget them; but the memory of their images haunted my dreams, and I knew that the only way to expel them from my mind was to use them as fictional fodder. Thus it was that I composed my first novel, *Beneath Arkham*, the publication of which brought me a modicum of fame.

Uncle Silas was not a literary man, and when I realized that as I approached manhood I felt a distinct disappointment. There he was, surrounded by Elmer Harrod's magnificent library, and he let the books gather dust, except for the summers when I visited, at which times I was often alone in the mammoth library devouring the nameless fictive lore. I don't think that Uncle Silas recognized that I was having less to do with him during my summer visits, or that my youthful high opinion of him had been tarnished when I realized that he did not share my love of literature. I was amazed and deeply grateful, of course, when he casually mentioned over one quiet dinner that he would bequeath me his house and its delirious contents, and it was then that I arranged for his portrait to be painted and replace the one of Harrod that hung over the fireplace in the living room. I never detected any strangeness in my uncle's demeanor, and his sudden suicide came as an unpleasant shock. I was ecstatic, of course, about leaving my small and pathetic apartment and moving into the mammoth house in Arkham, and yet everywhere I looked there were items that reminded me of the sad situation that had allowed me to move there. Still, the spacious library became my happy little world, and I devoted myself to the genre in which I plotted to become an active and popular voice, working on my own book by using Harrod's antiquated manual typewriter with which to compose my rough drafts. I felt a cool kind of communion knowing that the keys I pressed had felt the other fellow's touch. I could not help, at times, to look around me and laugh out loud at the world I had inherited; for as a television host, Harrod had crammed his abode with props from films and nightmarish gifts from fans and friends, so that his home came to resemble something out of Charles Addams. Yet for all of his outlandish behavior, his mugging before the camera as he filmed his campy introductions to forgotten horror films, I began to feel a kinship with Harrod, for he had loved weird literature. There were, on the walls, framed stills of Harrod with certain celebrities, many of them horror film players, but some few the actual authors of the books he had collected. I had discovered a large scrapbook in which Harrod had pasted some few newspaper articles or photos from the local media, who enjoyed writing about him around Halloween; and I was charmed by a photo of him reading an edition of Arthur Machen in Old Dethshill Cemetery. On a whim I decided to hunt for and peruse that very edition, which was easily found. As I opened the book, dry soil spilled onto my lap, and I suspected that the debris was graveyard dirt. In the newspaper cutting, Harrod was reading the book with the aid of a large flashlight – but that seemed wrong to me, and thus I was happy to find, in the back tool shed, an antique oil lamp. I was determined to journey into the graveyard that very night, book in hand, and read a story from it with the aid of lantern light.

I had turned a small room adjacent to the library into my bedroom and thus rarely visited the three upstairs bedrooms; but I was feeling a bit clownish that night and decided that I wanted to dress up for my first nighttide visit to Old Dethshill Cemetery, and so I climbed the carpeted stairs and went into Harrod's old room, which my uncle had preserved just as the horror host had left it and where many outlandish television costumes remained hanging in various closets. He had been as lean as I and about the same height, and so the tuxedo decorated with synthetic spider webs fitted rather well. Thus attired I took the lantern and edition of Machen and stepped into night's calm air. I could not see a moon, but the stars that dotted the cosmos seemed brighter than usual. The cemetery was just across the road from where I lived, and I felt a kind of joy as I climbed over its low stone wall and listened to the subtle sounds of the place. I was rather amazed at the aura of the place – it felt weirdly inhabited, although I was the lone individual there, and I heard no birds and glimpsed no scurrying vermin. I turned to look across the road at my home, where I had left some few lights on that illuminated various windows; and I marveled at the fantastic aura of the house in which I lived, at its sinister aspect that was aided by the rooftop gargoyles and other such paraphernalia with which Harrod had decorated it. I continued my exploration, walking through yellow grass that sometimes reached my knees, passing weed-choked markers and weathered tombstones on which names and dates had been erased by elemental time. I crossed over a creek that trickled through the cemetery and looked at the thickening trees that grew on the surrounding Arkham hills. There was no wind, yet the late August air was chilly, and so I stopped and lit my lantern, which aided sight but gave no warmth.

I heard a sudden wailing cry from somewhere in the trees just beyond me, a sound that seemed to summon nature's breath and coax a wind to exhale and thus stir up the scents of the place in which I lingered. Something in the sound of bestial cry touched my imagination, and I parted my mouth in imitation of the wail; and my noise was answered above me as a dark cloud melted and thus the moon that had been secreted behind it was exposed. I blinked as dead lunar light fell onto my eyes, as another sphere arose, as if from buried earth, small and delicate, with black pits where a human visage would wear eyes. A scarlet line, its mouth, parted, from which a patch of vapor poured forth, accompanied by a voice.

" *Ses yeux profonds sont faits de vide et de ténèbres…*"

The figure ceased its recitation and cocked its head. I watched as it hopped from the tabletop tomb and walked a few steps nearer, and as it approached I noticed the book it held. The young thing smiled and spoke again.

"I suppose you don't know French, judging from your dumb expression. Let me translate and sing the verse again, thus:

'Her eyes, made of the void, are deep and black;

Her skull, coiffured in flowers down the neck,

Sways slackly on the column of her back,

O charm of nothingness so madly decked!'

Delicious, is it not? And how clever of Luna to show her form just now, so as to aid with ghastly light. One should always read poetry by moonlight, don't you think?"

"Certainly, if the poet is Baudelaire."

"*Ah!* An educated soul." The voice was high and nasal, yet masculine. His eyes were concealed behind round black lenses of what looked like antique wire spectacles. His fantastic mauve hair was piled high upon his dome in thick tube-like coils, and moonlight shimmered on the crimson gloss with which his simpering lips had been coated. "I've been looking for mine kindred dead, for I've been told that many of us are planted here." He looked at me from behind his queer eyewear and spoke his name. "Randolph H. Carter, of Boston. And yes, I am ruefully related to the writer and man of mystery. Have you read his infamous book?"

"I've inherited a first edition, but I haven't looked at it yet. What was his mystery?"

"Oh, there are many, a multitude of riddles. What, for example, happened to his friend and mentor, Harley Warren, who was last seen with Randy on the day of Warren's disappearance? I actually know a direct relative of Warren's here in town, a fabulous painter who has a studio on French Hill. It was she, actually, who informed me of this place, for she often paints it and its denizens. Just now she is conjuring a life-size doppelganger of Obediah Carter, who was whispered to have been a wizard."

"That was his tomb you were standing on just now."

"Yes – I was drawn to it, but could not make out the inscription. I recognized him from his photograph, of course. Such a sinister face, don't you agree?" He began to walk but stumbled over a clump of weed. "Damn, this terrain is treacherous."

"Perhaps," I ventured, "you should remove the shades…"

"Don't be absurd." He cautiously moved away from me through tall dry grass, and so I held my lantern high so as to light our way as I followed. We both saw the tree at the same time, and I could not repress a shudder. "Some fool hanged himself on that tree last year." He turned and frowned at the expression on my face. "How sad you look – but then, who wouldn't, dressed like that. You look like some Gothic hobo. Well, I must depart, morning classes come so early. What are you reading?" I told him. "Ah," and he winked. "Best be on guard for the little people. This is so their demesne, one would imagine." He waved a petite hand and I watched him saunter toward the trees and vanish within their darkness, and suddenly I felt alone and vulnerable. Turning, I found my way homeward, climbed over the stone wall and examined my home. It looked a grotesque thing in the sallow moonlight, with its cupola, widow's walk and many gables. Lunar light feasted on the face of the gargoyle that Elmer Harrod had added as a feature to be seen when the house was filmed as part of the introductory footage of his television show, in which Elmer could be seen peering from a window, his face made up to resemble a rapacious ghoul. Standing as it did at the end of a dead end street on which most of the other houses were decayed and uninhabited, the Victorian pile wore an aura of desolation on this particular night. It looked very much a haunted house. And so it was, haunted by my lonely life, my strange imagination, my spectral dreams.

Entering my home, I went to the library and found the collection of horror stories by the original Randolph Carter, *The Attic Window and Others*, the first edition of which had been published by private hands some few years after the author's queer vanishing act in 1928. The book had caused a mild sensation due to hostile reviews, and a Carter cult had begun, centering primarily at Miskatonic University among the

Bohemians who were attracted to weird fiction, the occult and other such manifestations of morbidity. The commotion attracted the attention of a New York publisher, and a new edition containing additional stories sold very well, which led to the republication of Carter's novels, which were not as popular as his eerie early work. Settling into my cozy armchair, I cracked open the book and began to read, oblivious to the subtle keening of windsong that emanated from the nearby graveyard. Soon my eyes grew heavy, and my long day ended as I succumbed to slumber.

II.

It was a muted drumming that aroused me from the folds of dreaming that encased me like a filigree of spider web. Raising my hands, I pushed the debris of dream away and floated to my feet, watching as the book that had been on my lap drifted to the floor, where it lay open so as to reveal a curious symbol on its yellow leaf. I did not like the way that symbol oozed across the page, like a sentient spill of enchanted ink, and thus I reach down and closed the book, then took it up and pressed it to my breast as I listened again to the subterranean drumming. I followed the sound, which led me to the basement, a place I had not fully investigated on account of its damp chilliness, which I feared would trigger an asthma attack. I could not understand why the basement floor felt so soft beneath my feet. The rhythmic sensation of sound came from a small dark room, into which I drifted. A wrought iron sconce fastened to the wall held a squat black candle, and when I struck a match to its wick the room became subtly illuminated, enough so that I could see the panel in the wall that was slightly opened. I remembered reading in Elmer Harrod's journal of his finding a secret passageway in some section of the house – this must be the place of which he wrote. Grasping the thick black candle, I removed it from its sconce and pushed the panel with my shoulder, then stepped into the earthen passageway thus revealed. A current of air pushed at me, on which I could smell a remnant of ancient death; and this was perplexing because when I came to the end of the passageway I found myself confronted with a wall of moist yet solid earth, with no openings where a breeze might filter through. There was another sconce on the wall before me, and so I placed the candle in it and examined the curious emblem that had been etched into the surface of the wall, the familiar sign. One hand still pressed the book to my chest, but now I opened it and examined the similar sign that had stained its page. Although the beating of muted drums had softened, I sensed that they sounded still, from some place beyond the wall before me. I lifted my hand and followed the symbol's design with my finger, and as I did so the emblem in the book began to smoke. I shouted as the book crumbled into ash that sifted through my hand and drifted down, and then my blood froze as the heap of spilled ash began to rotate and rise until it formed a cowled figure that breathed upon me through a face that was hidden by its hood. A palsied hand arose and trembled before me, its fingers resembling bloated grave worms that seemed to hunger for my soul. One of those soft moist fingers pressed against my forehead and began to etch a symbol onto my flesh. I pushed away from the thing, against the wall of earth, that wall that took me within its substance as if it were a pit within cemetery sod. The cowled figured bent toward me as the pounding I had heard filled my head, the noise that I knew was the beating of my heart. A glimmer of candlelight caught the countenance within the hood, a face that was familiar; for I had seen its likeness in a photograph that had been attached to the tomb slab of Obediah Carter.

III.

I pushed the dream away and laughed as I stretched in the library armchair with Carter's book of weird tales in my lap. The clock told me that it was mid-morning, and yet the muted light that sifted through the window was quite thick, so I got to my feet and went to open the front door, where I was confronted with a blanket of fog. Old Dethshill Cemetery was hidden from view, yet I could *feel* its palpable presence, and I could hear its subtle sounds, its never-ending stirrings and rustlings and whisperings. Perhaps a part of my mind was still lost in dreaming, or my horror writer's imagination was working subconsciously – for some of the sounds I heard were surely imaginary. It amused me that I was becoming obsessed with the neighboring necropolis, and I wanted to visit it more often. There was only one thing within it that tainted my fondness for the place – that bleached emblem of my uncle's lunacy and suicide. If that was removed, all would be well, and I could linger within the cemetery often and let it arouse my creativity, as it had inspired my dreaming. It was the thickness of the fog that coaxed me toward resolution. I went to the garden shed and found the can of petrol that was there, then slipping garden gloves over my hands I carried the can through the fog, over the low stone wall and into the cemetery. The atmosphere was thick with weird foreboding, which thrilled me. I wanted to remember the sensation so as to describe it in my next book, in which I would evoke the phantoms of this haunted place. It was funny, I felt as I tramped through the fog that I had entered yet another dream in which I floated past rotting slates of stone and tabletop tombs that invited one to stop, recline, and rest one's mortal bones. "Perchance to dream," I whispered, reflecting on Hamlet's soliloquy regarding the dreams one might experience in death. I had a hunch that death was not the end of the soul, and Old Dethshill Cemetery seemed to somehow verify that intuition – for this was a place that lived with a sentience all its own, unearthly though it be.

I moved through mauve fog until the monstrous tree stood before me. The fog contained a kind of brightness that illuminated every awful aspect of the fiendish thing on which my uncle had found extinction – the sickly hue of its pallid bark, the softness of that bark and the anomalous symbols carved thereon. Seeing those symbols inspired me to shudder, for they were too similar to something I seemed to half-remember from a recent dream. I did not like them, nor did I like the unnatural vines that issued out of the tree's sinister branches – those creepy vines that, in this fog, resembled alien veins of something that might exist beneath the ocean's depths. Utterly repulsed, I opened the can of gasoline and splashed its contents all over the monstrous tree, and then I removed my gloves and lit a long wooden match, which I tossed to the bleached thing which burst into flame. Billowing smoke was concealed by the thickness of fog, but the stench that issued from the burning thing was so vile and pungent that

I was glad that I lived alone on that dead end street. Laughing like a lunatic, I spat at the flaming horror and fled.

I stayed away from the cemetery for some time, slightly unnerved by my actions and not desirous to witness their effect. I had acted on impulse, and it now seemed a mad and careless performance. To take my mind off the matter, I plunged into the writing of a new book of short stories. A friend in New York who operated a small press devoted to weird fiction had expressed an interest in a collection of my tales, which he wanted to bring out as a limited edition hardcover. His books were beautifully produced and designed, and so the idea thrilled me and I began to write the first of five new stories that would see their first publication in this new collection. It was natural, I suppose, that the first tale on which I worked was set in Old Dethshill Cemetery, which I renamed. Writing about the place seemed to weave a kind of enchantment over me and made me want to visit the place again. Perhaps now that the devil tree had been destroyed I could enjoy the place without qualms. Taking a break from writing one day, I rose and went out the front door so as to stand on the porch and observe the neighboring graveyard, and I saw a familiar figure traipsing among the high grass. I watched him for a little while, and he suddenly turned to me and waved. I returned his salute but was grateful that he did not venture toward the house, for I was not in a social mood. But as I watched him I had decided to use Randolph H. Carter as a character in my tale, turning him into a delirious fop whom I would call "Samuel," a creature of curious heritage. This inspired a new direction for my story, in which I conjured forth some of Arkham's whispered legends and history, and my imagination was so stimulated that this became the book's lengthiest work. The writing of the book was pure joy, and I was amazed at how quickly the work poured from me. In no time at all, the book was a published reality, in a limited edition of three hundred illustrated copies, fifty of which were bought by a shop in Arkham that specialized in horror and fantasy, histories of witchcraft and so on. Invited to the shop to sit and sign my book for the students who seemed to be its chief audience, I went first to Elmer Harrod's bedroom and found the vampire cloak that he had often donned before the television camera, and I used some of my inheritance left by my uncle to purchase a handsome tuxedo. On my way to the signing I stopped at a floral shop and bought a beautiful white rose to slip into my buttonhole, and it pleased me when the florist recognized me from a short article that had been written about my book in the local paper. The evening proved quite successful, many books were sold and signed, and I was happy. The event was reaching its conclusion when young Carter entered the shop and purchased a copy of my book. I smiled at him as I signed.

"Inscribe, please – but not to me; sign it to Julia Warren. Are you done here? Let me take you out for a small meal, you must be famished." I signed my signature and rose to take my leave, thanking the shop owner and congratulating her on the night's success. Carter slipped the book into a shoulder bag and motioned me to follow him. I was surprised when we stepped outside to find a cab waiting for us in front of the store, and I followed Carter as he stepped inside the vehicle. How strangely he smiled at me as he removed a length of black cloth from his bag. "Indulge me, Hayward," he sighed as he smoothed the cloth over his knee, "but I have a little adventure planned. No, don't frown – you'll enjoy this and be amused, I promise. I'm going to tie this cloth around your eyes, and I think you'll be pleasantly surprised when my mystery is revealed. It's all linked to your book, you see, and to your outlandish use of my persona in that one story, which flattered as much as it insulted – do you really find me so frivolous? You barely know me! There, the cloth is secure. No peeking. You mentioned in that newspaper interview that you've not seen much of Arkham town – which is your own fault, since you insist on burying yourself in your outlandish house, glued to your keyboard. Tonight you will be acquainted with a lovely witch-town haunt. Lovely, I knew you'd be a sport."

"How do you know my name? I never told you."

"Oh, we know many secrets, dear boy."

"We?" I heard him snigger as he touched his shoulder to mine, and the peculiar odor of his tubes of hair wafted to me. I frowned and asked, "Is that your real hair, or is it a wig?"

"Don't be stupid. If it were a wig it would look more natural. Sit still, Hayward. Okay, cabbie, proceed." The car began to move, and thus I sat blindfolded and just a bit bemused. My life *had* reached a point of rather tedious routine. I was a bookish introvert who relished silence and solitude. I had written my book because of my keen fondness for the weird fiction genre; that the possible popularity of my book would debauch my privacy was not something I had anticipated. A part of me welcomed this sudden misadventure with this perverse stranger who seemed to want to be my friend. I assured myself that I would be cautious in handling any threads of popularity that came my way – but then I laughed quietly at the idea of caution, for here I was in a taxi cab, blindfolded and off to some secret rendezvous!

Carter, as we rode, was more talkative than usual, and I sensed that he was trying to distract my attention and thus disrupt any attempt to determine our direction. Smiling and silent, I listened to his babble, until at last the car stopped and I was guided (still blindfolded) onto a path of gravel. The cloth was loosened and I reached for it and removed it from before my eyes as the cab rushed from us; and although I had once more obtained sight, darkness was still my domain – for we stood in a slim alley between what looked like two antiquated warehouses, one of which had a steep and tilting flight of weathered wooden steps, to which I was led.

"It can't be safe, climbing those."

"As long as it's not raining there is little danger. Hang on to the railing if you're feeling cautious. I've climbed them often and they are perfectly secure despite their great age – but then the past is far more solid than this present plastic age, my dear." We climbed the many steps to a small platform and Carter pushed open the door before us, allowing a variety of smells, among which was the odor of turpentine, to assail our nostrils. Entering a spacious candlelit chamber, I soon realized that I was in an artist's studio, although one that looked as if it belonged to a distant era. Antique furnishings stood here and there, as did a number of ancient brass candelabras, on some few of which a number of candles furnished moving amber light. One entire wall was made of mirrors, and a curious concealed electric light effect made this wall appear to be composed of shimmering liquid, like some perpendicular pool in which one could watch wavering reflections. The strange young man tilted near to me and whispered, "This is one of my very special haunts."

I looked around at the various large canvases that leaned against walls or were propped on easels, and then I experienced a freezing of the blood as my eyes fell upon a life-size reproduction of the awful tree that had once stood in the neglected necropolis and on which my uncle had ended his life. I could not resist the compulsion to go to the enormous canvas and touch it, to study the structure of the outré tree, so perfectly replicated; and I felt a kind of sickness as I studied its sinister pale vines that seemed like the writhing veins of some unfathomable chimera. "It's no longer there," spoke a husky voice from one corner of the studio. "Someone has destroyed it, there's just a pile of white ashes where it used to stand." Turning to face the speaker, I confronted the small middle-aged woman who advanced through the flickering candlelight. Her gray hair was worn short, and her black clothes spotted with paint and other stains. "It was your relative who hanged himself from it, wasn't it?"

"It was."

"And you who destroyed it?"

I turned to gaze at the painting again. "Yes."

Carter joined us, his expression dark. "This is Julia Morgan Warren, grandniece of Harley Warren, the friend of my ancestor. And this, dear Julia, is Hayward Phelps, author, haunter of graveyards – and avenger." He reached into his shoulder bag and brought forth my book. "This is the collection of fantastic fiction that he has penned under the curious name of Deth Carter Hill – you really are obsessed with that place, aren't you, old thing? I suppose I should be honored that my fabulous persona inspired the creation of your lead story's main character. Of course, your fictive portrayal is an exaggeration although not quite a parody." I could not help but laugh, for the absurdity of my being there and listening to such talk came to me. It was like having entered one of my own weird tales, and I liked it very much.

The painter nodded her thanks for the book, wiping her hands on an old rag before taking it from her friend. "You wrote this in Elmer Harrod's haunted house?"

"Yes, which I inhabited eighteen months ago. It was bequeathed to me by my uncle, may he rest in peace. It's really a remarkable place, containing as it does all of the belongings of the horror host. I've been visiting it since my teenage years, and it has never lost its allure. It never occurred to me that I would someday be able to live within its walls."

"Your uncle purchased it – from whom?"

"I never knew. He never said. I tried to discover the circumstances, but apparently my uncle destroyed all papers concerning the transaction. All very mysterious. I've been unable to find any of Harrod's relations, who might want to claim some of his library – some few of the books are quite rare and valuable. From all I've learned about Harrod, he never made any mention of family, and none of his kindred ever came to call. He lived in a world of his making, alone mostly, although he did enjoy entertaining stay-over guests. Vincent Price stayed there one weekend. I think he and Harrod shared an interest in art." As I spoke, I studied some of Miss Warren's artistic tools which lay on a table near us. One item was especially attractive, and so I took it up to examine it.

"Isn't that lethal tool amazing," Carter opined. "The handle is ivory, as you can see, with elegant decorative work in silver. Be cautious opening it, for the blade is very sharp. It was part of a Victorian mortuary kit that Julia purchased, and must have helped numberless corpses with their last shave."

"This may interest you," spoke the painter, motioning that I should follow her to a large canvas on which she had painted the house I had inherited, catching to perfection the Gothic aura of the place. Yet she had enhanced its curious quality with clever touches, such as the way in which the trees she had painted contained a kind of sentience, or the way in which shadows seemed to peer from places in the stormy sky. "I was able to enter it just once, when I was young. Harrod held a party for budding young artists of the area – he did indeed have an interest in art. I confess I became obsessed with the house and its neighboring graveyard, both of which have become the repeated topics of my work. There is a strange appetite for works of the house among locals – strange because we find the place compelling and yet something about it disturbs us. Perhaps it's that dead-end street and the fact that the other houses have been vacated, adding to the idea that the area is some kind of shunned locality. Haven't you noticed it, how everything seems subtly *tainted* in the area, touched and twisted by some mysterious force? A force that attracts as much as it repulses?"

"What I feel – it's a force from the past. Everything there seems rooted to some bygone era, the houses, that bewitching graveyard and those who have been planted in it. The grave for your distant ancestor, Carter, really affected me, to the point where his persona has invaded my dreaming. I find it all so strangely attractive. I hate this unimaginative modern age. Gawd, the life I was 'living' before I came into my inheritance, living in a small yet expensive apartment, slaving away as prep cook and dishwasher at a job that so exhausted me that I had no energy for anything once I got home from work. It was a non-life."

Carter moved away from us as I spoke and went to gaze at another work of art. "He was a dynamic force, old Obediah – and your conjuring of him is magnificent, dear Julia." Miss Warren and I went to join him, and I was indeed impressed and mesmerized. The painting was a huge life-size representation of the ancient warlock, and the light from the nearest candelabra revealed that the paint was still fresh and wet. The face was nearly identical to that of the miniature on the tomb, with the one exception of the queer distortion of the right eye. I thought perhaps the paint there had somehow melted or run amok, but as I stepped closer to the canvas I saw that the disfigurement was deliberate. "Ah, yes," Carter sighed, "*the blemished eye.* There have been some few Arkham families that have suffered individuals born with such an eye, linking them to whispers of witchcraft. Family legend has it that Obediah owned such an orb, although he had the fault corrected in all portraits painted of him." I turned and studied Carter's pale face, the painted lips, the dark spectacles. Laughing, he removed the eyewear and revealed two normal eyes of pale gray. "Not a hereditary ailment, I'm happy to report." Frowning at the candlelight, he returned his spectacles to his face. "Anyway, Julia has restored nature and portrayed him with his imperfection. She's good, isn't she? You should have her paint you, Hayward, a lovely portrait to be used in place of author's photograph for some future book."

"I can see the family resemblance," I replied as I peered at the painting. "Despite your ridiculous tresses. You're much younger than he is here depicted, far leaner; but it's there in his expression, a kind of superior cynicism. What is it that sets your blood above us low mortals, Carter? What have you personally accomplished in life?"

He seemed dumbfounded by my sudden criticism. "I appreciate art and literature."

"Is that all?"

"It's enough for now. As you have remarked, I'm wonderfully young, a mere child, really. Adulthood, from what I've seen of it, is hell. I have decided to live a life that is exquisitely Bohemian. Like you, I've come into my inheritance, and I delight in the freedom it allows."

The woman touched my hand. "It's nice to have you venture out of that old house and brave the public. I suppose your publisher talked you into it, to help promote the book. We are happy to become more acquainted with such an enigmatic creature."

"I beg your pardon?"

"You've been a mystery ever since first moving to Arkham and claiming Elmer Harrod's haunted house. Yes, we still call it, and always will. That marvelous place has such a hold on local imaginations because of seeing it on television week after week. And the place gained an additional sinister aura after Elmer's grotesque corpse was discovered in the graveyard. I used to hang out at that graveyard just to be near the house and try to observe its inhabitant. I was but a child when my family settled in Arkham fifty-eight years ago, and that house has always beguiled me. There was usually a buzz of activity there, as if Elmer couldn't stand to be inside it alone. He used to host an annual Halloween party for local kids, but I wasn't allowed to attend until I was well into my teens. That place was never quiet – that's my memory of it, there was almost always some kind of action, be it the student film crews from Miskatonic that were hired to film Elmer's weekly television spot, or entertaining his B-film guests. That placed bubbled with life. It's quite another matter with you."

I laughed. "And shall remain so. What I adore about the residence is its sense of solitude, the feeling there that I have escaped not only the world but time itself. It's not a sense that comes over me just because of antique furnishings and endless quietude – it's something...other. I never see anyone, except now and then the homeless vagrants who seek shelter in the vacated houses. Living in Harrod's house is like...living in a book, I guess that's how I can best explain it. It delights me with a feeling of real escape from insipid reality. I need no other realm, which I guess is why I've not explored much of Arkham. My existence before this – was no existence at all, just dull routine, day after relentless day. I was stifled, damned by a non-life that lacked art and imagination. My one escape, besides the library books I devoured, was to visit my uncle for two weeks every summer, curled up in his library with the astounding Elmer Harrod library, watching the collection of Harrod's homemade films, exploring that house of secrets when left alone within it. I would pine, for the rest of the year, to be there again, even when my maturity dimmed my youthful admiration for my uncle, who was rather a blasé individual with no real grasp of life or art. Now I can dwell within that magick realm for the rest of my life, so why should I seek to roam anywhere else, even in a town of dark legend such as Arkham? Of late I have developed a new interest in the town, but it's related to my interest in the Carter family, and my use of their history in a series of novels I hope to write." I smiled at Carter. "How strange, then, to accompany you, the freakish remnant of that ancient line. Despite your absurdity, I can sense *something* about you – some rare element that is disguised by your outlandish appearance and adolescent ways. Your two ancestors fascinate me, more and more, they and their legends. They both vanished under queer circumstances, right?" The others glanced at each other, and the small woman smiled.

"Oh, we know as little as anyone else. It was ages ago, all of that – ancient history, myth and legend." Judging from the expression on her face, Julia seemed not to care that I knew she was lying. I returned her feeble smile.

"And yet you've unearthed the furtive secret of Obediah and his blemished eye." I pointed to the painting of the sorcerer. "There may be other secrets just waiting to be exposed, if only one knew where to hunt." I winked at them, still smiling; and although they tried to keep their smiles, I detected something secretive and unspoken in the way they tried not to look at me, the emotions they were determined to conceal. I saw it, underneath their curving lips and in the shadows of their eyes.

Young Carter blinked at me. "Well, I promised you dinner. Let us depart. Will you join us, Julia? No? My dear, I *never* see you eat! However do you nourish yourself?"

"My art sustains me, Randy." She looked at him for one mysterious moment, and then she turned her eyes to mine, and I imagined that they contained some secret that I was somehow supposed to understand.

IV.

Our taxi brought us to my haunted house, and we sat for some few silent moments before I opened the door. "Would you care to come in?"

"That would be amazing!" Randolph enthused, taking out a billfold and paying the driver. We stood and watched the cab drive away, and then he turned to peer into the graveyard. The moon was very high above us, and the wooded area of the cemetery and the forested hills beyond it swayed softly in the evening wind. From somewhere among the trees or tombs something cried in eerie ululation.

"That's odd," I spoke. "I've never witnessed any birds in that place, day or night."

"Was it a bird?" asked the lad's faraway voice.

I shrugged and turned to walk the path to the porch steps, with Carter behind me as I climbed them to the door, although he paused momentarily to tilt his head and watch the gargoyle that Harrod had attached to the building's roof. I unlocked the door and waited for him to preceed me inside, and then I took his jacket and hung it on the coat rack. "Come on into the library. I'll just pop into the kitchen; I have some excellent coffee." Entering the library, I motioned for him to either sit in one of the many comfortable chairs or prowl so as to study titles on the shelves that had been built into the walls; then I left him and went to the small kitchen, where I brewed coffee and selected a variety of cookies. From some distant place outside I heard a repetition of an inhuman cry from Old Dethshill Cemetery, and as the coffee was brewing I opened the door leading outside and stepped onto the stone walkway. I listened – and when the queer cry came again I parted my lips and uttered a replication of the sound. The air seemed to grow a little chilly as the sky darkened and the earth rumbled faintly with some deeply buried hill noises beyond the field of death. How strangely one's imagination can play with one. I imagined that night's silence transmuted, became quiet yet attentive – like an animal observing its prey. The bubbling of percolation came from the kitchen, and I returned inside and shut the antique door, yet I could not shake off a brooding sense of disturbance. "How the horror writer's imagination loves to spook itself," I told the cookies, chuckling. Preparing the tray, I picked it up and returned to the library, where I saw my guest return one book to a shelf and remove another. He turned to glance at me as I set the tray on a small table, and then he opened the book. We watched the particles of debris that fell from it to the floor.

"That's the third book I've opened that has dirt between the pages. What the hell?"

I shrugged. "Both Harrod and Uncle Silas were wont to take books into the graveyard." I pointed to a framed newspaper photo on one wall of the horror host in ghoulish garb, posing with an edition of Blackwood as he perched upon a tombstone. "I think perhaps one or both had a habit of sprinkling cemetery sod into the books. It's certainly strange."

Carter returned the book to its place on the shelf and sauntered about the room. "There's a lovely ambiance here, what with the soft light, the antique furnishings, and that delicious aroma of old books. I can understand why you don't like leaving this realm. However, I'm just slightly disappointed with the house – I expected it to feel more haunted. I mean, the previous two tenants were so queer, no one really knew what Harrod did with his private time – he seems to have spent so much effort in not being alone in this house, which is so suggestive. He used to hint that there were secret passageways beneath the house or some such thing, but he never showed these tunnels to anyone because he protested that if he did they would no longer be 'secret.' He was rarely alone: film crews made up of students from Miskatonic, constant houseguests, visiting fans who were treated to tea and tall tales. His entire persona was founded on performance, and the show never ended; even his death was pure theatre." He smiled wickedly. "And then your enigmatic uncle did quite the reverse and never entertained, except apparently yourself when you were an adolescent. He seems a very strange old duck, your uncle."

"Uncle Silas was a loner, certainly. A strange man, as you say, but not, in the final assessment, an interesting one. He either made or inherited a lot of money when he was young; I never knew the story of his wealth. I certainly didn't expect him to leave everything to me, but perhaps he didn't notice how critical I had become of him as I matured. He knew I loved this house and its library, and he encouraged my early efforts at writing. His big love in life was watching horror films, and that was fine when I was a kid, but…" I looked at him and returned his smile. "How amusing, though, for you to speak of how odd *my* relative was. I've read your namesake's book, with its brief biographical introduction. The original Randolph Carter – now there's an enigma! A mystic, people called him, but what exactly does that mean? Was he some kind of occultist, as Obediah Carter is rumored to have been?"

The young creature's voice was very quiet in reply. "Obediah was much more than that." He stood regarding me with a peculiar expression on his face as the room's soft light glimmered on his black spectacles. Reaching into his shoulder bag, he produced a small book that was bound in red cloth, and he stared at the thing for some silent moments before handing it to me. "That's the diary of Randolph W. Carter, written before he became middle-aged and disillusioned, before the incident with Julia's ancestor, with whom Carter lived and studied until the night of mystery and doom. You look lost, Hayward. I thought you were familiar with that other Randolph's history."

"I know some of the legend from studying your family history for fictional purposes. There's not really much solid biographical information on him, although he supposedly hinted of things in his short fiction. I've never bothered reading his novels, which are rumored to be poor and unimaginative."

"No, they're fascinating, and proved popular in his day. His current reputation is stupidly tied to the mystery of his disappearance and little else, although his books are mostly back in print. I grew up in a family of staid Bostonians who were slightly embarrassed by family ties to Arkham and its 'mystics.' Family legend hints that no one paid much attention to Randy's estate, although there are now doubts as to how vigorously the family was sought by the queer fellow in New Orleans who had been named in the will as literary and financial executor. Randy's early work was a shunned subject when I grew up because it's tied too intimately to his link with magick and madness, and with Arkham. They don't like Arkham in Boston, and the family was never forgiven for returning here and disappearing somewhere near the ruins of the family's ancestral mansion just outside of town. You've noticed that that diary is almost exclusively a record of time spent in cemeteries. You're looking for mention of Old Dethshill Cemetery, aren't you? You won't find it. It seems implausible that Randy never visited it, so many of our kindred dead have been dumped there. His story, 'Return of the Warlock,' is said to have been inspired by Edmund Carter, a sensational sorcerer who barely escaped hanging and whose secret journal Randy had found in some ancestral attic – and it so disturbed him that he had the pages sealed!"

I was half-listening to his prattling as I scanned the pages in the small book I held, the history of Carter's seeking lost and forgotten ancestors in the burying grounds of New England. More interesting than his historical pursuit, however, was his obvious affection for these fields of death. The combination of my visitor's tale, told in his faint voice, with the imaginative lines of his forebear's diary, so beautifully expressed, filled me with an overwhelming desire to dream and write. I sensed the beginning of my own first novel, one that would relate the history of the Carter family and its ties to witch-haunted Arkham. I would have to alter the name and much of that history – that would be part of the creative fun of the work – but locals would certainly guess the origin of the family whose dark history I would relate. I looked up as Carter walked away from me and to a window. I said, "I suppose your family changed its tune about Carter's books once the novels began to sell again."

"That was part of it. We heard from some old writer in Providence, who had saved a packet of letters that Randy had written him. The guy wanted to reprint some of Randy's horror stories in a handsome hardcover edition and include the best of the letters as an appendix. He had sought out my grandfather's permission. That was followed by someone wanting to write a biographical novel about Randy's weird mysticism and his vanishing into the Arkham hills – and that Grandpa would not allow. But the family sensed a growing interest in our weird one, and began to think about the possible financial assets such a thing might develop. You know," spoke his low faint voice as he pushed aside a curtain and peered into outer darkness through black lens, "Randy wasn't the only Carter to vanish somewhere in the hills of Arkham. Another of the clan went missing under mysterious circumstances in 1781. Less than ten years later Obediah was born under what were whispered to be savage conditions linked to alchemy. God, what a heritage!" I studied his slim feminine figure, the tight-fitting black apparel, the impossible hair piled in coils on his head. This was the first time I had studied that hair in decent light, and I marveled that human hair could look so artificial, more like vines or tubes than anything else. The more I stared at it the more I was certain that it was not his natural growth but rather some clever synthetic attachment.

I didn't know how to respond to his talk, and so I remained silent as he moved from the window and to another wall shelf lined with books. I watched as he removed a volume of Henry James's ghost stories and raised the book to his delicate nostrils, and I imagined him shutting his eyes as he sucked in the old book's fragrance, even though those eyes were concealed behind the dark lens of his absurd glasses. Opening the book, Carter allowed some particles of dirt to fall into one hand. His face darkened as he stared at the rubble in his palm, and then he brought that palm to his mouth and touched the debris with his tongue, as from some distant place outside a thing cried to twilight.

V.

My guest insisted that he wanted to walk home, and so I stood on the porch and watched him cross the road and enter into Old Dethshill Cemetery. He turned to me, waved and smiled, and did a little jig among the stones. He was a silly creature, but I was getting to like him. I returned his wave and then returned into my home, happy to be alone. I had not yet removed Harrod's heavy cloak, and so I climbed the stairs to his room and began to undress, breathing easier as the tie was removed and the shirt's top button released. Standing in my underwear, I put the discarded clothes into the closet and then sat upon the dead man's massive bed, which proved extremely comfortable. Because I had closed all of the vents in the upstairs section of the house, the room was chilly; and when I reached down to open a bedside bureau I smiled to find a pair of yellow pajamas.

Pulling on bottoms, I was happy to find them a perfect fit for me, and the thick material was certainly comfortable. I pulled the top part of the pajamas over my head and reclined on Harrod's bed, contemplating his possible sex life. Most of his visitors, from what I could ascertain, had been men. Perhaps he had been queer – or perhaps, like me, he had no interest in sex, preferring to be alone with his books and dreams. I rose and turned off the overhead light, then went to open the curtains of one window and thus allow moonlight to beam into the cozy room. Returning to the bed, I rested my shoulders and head on a pile of pillows and closed my eyes.

In dream, I returned to Miss Warren's studio. My thoughts on sexual matters must have tainted my dreams, for the small woman was nude as she danced before her painting of the sinister pale tree that once lived among the graveyard tombs. As she danced, her painted image began to writhe behind her, unwinding its tendrils of vine so that they embraced her neck and coiled atop her head, reminding me of something I could not clearly recollect. Someone linked my arm, and I saw that a robed figure stood beside me; and when its black eyes turned to wink at me, I saw Carter's pale face beneath the hood. How strangely he smiled at me as he led me to the naked woman and her painting, through which we walked. Holding tightly to my hands, they led me in a ritual danse around the writhing tree, and then they came near to embrace me and kiss my eyes. When they drifted away from me, their mouths moved but I could hear no uttered communication – the dream was entirely silent, except for the sound of deep breathing, which I assumed must be coming from my sleeping form, an infiltration of reality into the realm of phantasy. Each took hold of one of my hands and led me through the tall grass, past black rotting tombstones, just beyond an ivied mausoleum. I saw what looked to be an open grave, but as I was pulled into it I found that there were earthen steps leading to unseen depths. For the first time, I was aware of fragrance – or rather, stench, as we stepped through a dark passageway underground. I peered through the darkness to a blacker form before us, one that caused my bones to shudder with fear and from which the stench of death weaved through the air and froze my brain.

I awakened.

40

Moonbeams had been replaced by misty morning light. A bird warbled from a tree outside the window. I rose and stretched, and then remembered a part of the house that I had yet to visit. Exiting the room, I climbed the steps that led to the widow's walk, and despite my uneasiness with heights, I stepped out on the platform and to its rail of white wood. Why this section of the house existed I did not understand, for there was nothing to gaze at except the thickly wooded area of Old Dethshill Cemetery and the forested hills beyond it. I had not realized until then the immense thickness of the growth of trees in the area, especially in the graveyard. The burying ground looked utterly desolate, a lonely and forsaken realm indeed. I looked down to the ground just below me, and that was a mistake for I was seized by a sudden fit of vertigo. Dizzy and afraid, I backed to the door and re-entered my home. I went to the landing and down the stairs, to the library, which was now the room I most occupied, into which I had moved a small cot and much of my wardrobe. Dressing, I went to the kitchen and prepared a light breakfast, and as I sat at the table and devoured my omelet, I studied the door that led to the basement, another place I had yet to fully investigate. I remembered the afternoon my uncle had taken me down there and showed me the entrance to the secret passage, and how I was too fearful to step with him into that sequestered place. Dumping my dishes into the sink, I went to the library and got the antique lantern, then returned to the kitchen and walked down the skinny steps that took me to the basement. The area was smaller than I remembered it being, and I easily found that portion of the wall that, after a switch was flipped, slid open so as to reveal the tunnel hewn out of the earth, which was much more spacious than I had expected it to be. The floor was not just earth but some kind of finished material. My lantern's glow fell upon an object heaped at one place, and I reached to pick up the hooded robe, the material of which was smooth and slightly damp. I pushed my arms through the sleeves and pulled the hood over my head, then continued my journey through the tunnel. A slight and chilly breeze pushed at me, and I noticed some few vents built into the wall, and also fixtures that were apparently meant to hold torches, which made me feel that the tunnel was a thing of the deep past, long predating the structure that had been built above it. Attracted by a slim

41

recess that moved away from the main tunnel, I entered and followed it, sensing that it was slightly inclined and taking me to higher ground. Finally the darkness grew less so, and I found myself confronted with steps of sod that rose toward an opening through which daylight filtered. Climbing the smooth steps, I entered Old Dethshill Cemetery, at a place near a mausoleum where the growth of trees was less vigorous and allowed dawn to illuminate the area. How strange, that to stand among those markers of death in daylight was far creepier than to do so at night. The graveyard, in daylight, had a kind of presence that darkness clothed. It felt dangerous and – *hungry*. I fancied that it longed to devour my soul. Tearing the robe off me and letting it fall to the ground, I turned out the lantern's flame and found my way home.

Never had my haunted house felt more welcoming, a safe harbor. I wanted, however, to capture the feeling of fear that I had just experienced, and so I rushed into the library and began to write, composing a kind of prose poem that I hoped I could turn into the opening chapter of the novel I intended to write about the cemetery and the Carters who were interred therein. I don't know how long I sat there, at my desk, scribbling. Slight hunger reminded me of the time, and so I went to the kitchen and built myself a massive sandwich, which I washed down with some glasses of milk. I saw from the wall clock, and from the shadows outside the window, that afternoon was darkening into early dusk. Returning to the library, I sat on the sofa with one lamp spreading its soft light over the book I had decided to reread that evening, *The Attic Window and Others*. Carter's prose had a style all its own, very literary and rather rococo, a manner that proved mesmerizing and caught one's imagination. His ideas, for the most part, were not all that original, but his handling of them was evocative, and he had the ability to conjure a secret mythos of terror as no modern author I had read. I must have eventually dozed because I was startled awake by the sound of something's shrill cry in the graveyard next door. I looked around me at the trappings that had been bequeathed me by my uncle, and that had come his way through the inheriting of Elmer Harrod's "haunted house," as the locals were determined to name it. What an absurd, adolescent realm I had adopted as my own, and yet how easily I fitted into it. I realized there was very little of myself within the house, of my personality; for I was not much of a collector of anything before I had inherited the place and my belongings were few. I did not feel the need, now that I had some wealth, to buy things so as to add a bit of my presence into the place. Rather, I would let the atmosphere of spookiness guide my life as an author, and grow old with the harmless horrors thus evoked. I smiled to realize that I was, for the first time, happy and content. Harrod's haunted house was my safe harbor. Actually, it was the graveyard that was truly haunted, by phantoms of the past and their intrigues. One such phantom might have been the author of the book I had been reading, although there was no record of his ever having haunted Old Dethshill Cemetery. Looking around the room, I espied the antique lantern that had inspired me to read books within the graveyard on certain nights, as had Harrod and my uncle before me. It had been some little while since I had ventured into the burying ground with a book, and one very appropriate title was now in hand. Thus inspired, I stood and grasped the lantern, then went to the front door and stepped into the gulf of night, where a star-studded abyss yawned above me. Setting the book and lamp on a porch swing, I found my box of matches and lit the lantern's wick, and then I retrieved my objects and stepped down the porch, along the walkway, across the road and into the waiting necropolis.

Yes. It was *this spectral place* that was truly eerie, not my happy home. I could feel it all around me and hear it in the low moan of wind, and I could see it as my lantern light fell on the tall dead grass that looked like paper-thin tendrils reaching for me. I beheld it in the mournful swaying of the thick growth of trees. Below one section of those trees a spectre stood dead still among the weathered slabs, an eidolon in white that raised an arm and motioned me to join her. I went to Julia and took her proffered hand. In her other arm she cradled a box of fragrant wood on which elder symbols had been carved, emblems that I seemed to remember from snatches of dreaming. The small woman stood near to where Obediah Carter's weed-choked slab caught patches of pale moonlight on its hoary stone. Raising my lantern, I tried to comprehend the thing that reclined upon that slab, the creature that moved a petite hand into the nearest earth and clutched a fistful of cemetery sod. I watched that hand sail from the soil to a shadowed visage and let the debris sift through parting fingers into a waiting mouth. The wind arose, as did the being on the slab; and with him raised a cloud of mist that aped a human shape, like some shadow conjoined to the breathing mortal who gazed at me. Carter's face had never looked so blanched, all color leaked from the texture of his skin. I almost wanted to laugh, because his almost-ghoulish appearance reminded me of how Elmer Harrod sometimes looked in his ghoulish makeup when filmed in this same place. The young man before me smiled, as if he understood what I was thinking, and as his lips curled a little bit of dirt slipped from one corner of his mouth. He chortled, and the coils piled atop his dome shook, unwound, and fell to his feminine shoulders. I watched them sway in the wind – although something in their movement seemed too vigorous for the force of wind that touched us. Julia pressed her little body against mine and pressed her mouth to my ear.

"We are happy to have you here, to share the gift of nourishment. Oh, Hayward, you'll never be alone again." She opened the aromatic box and I saw the pile of white ash within it, on top of which was her Victorian mortuary straight razor that I had so admired in her studio. Sensuously, she inhaled the contents of the box, and then she dipped one hand into its contents and pinched a bit of ash. Moving from me, she glided to Carter and rubbed the ashes onto his soiled mouth, and his tongue played over her fingers as his tubes of colorless hair swayed and lengthened. The lad shuddered spasmodically for some few moments as I held the lantern high enough to clearly study his countenance – and thus I witnessed his black spectacles as they tilted on his vibrating head and slipped partially down his nose; and I saw his eyes, one of which was newly blemished. My blood became like ice.

The artist bent low and placed the box onto the ground, clutched the razor within it and stood erect. I watched as she lifted her arms, as the sleeves of her gown slid down so that her scars were revealed, some of which she kissed. Then her mouth moved to one of the tube-like extensions of Carter's impossible hair as the puny fingers of one hand pushed his spectacles back in place over his eyes. Portions of his hair, the tresses of which had lengthened so that they reached his waist, wound like amorous things around the woman's wounded arms. I watched, nauseated, as she sliced into one arm with razor blade, and I fought sickness as a tube of hair lifted to the wound and pushed

44

through it into Julia's arm. Dark fluid began to flow inside the tube-like extension.

Carter raised a hand in which he held dirt, bent back his head and opened his mouth, from which there issued a familiar wailing sound. He turned his hand over and let the soil fill his eager mouth, and I shivered as the tubes that extended from his scalp grew dark with the fragments that filtered through them. Julia laughed and the tube that had entered her arm filled with flowing debris that washed into her upraised limb. "More," she begged, "more. Nourish me. My arm hungers." My knees, weakened, bent and I fell onto them. This caught their attention, and the creatures turned to me. "Hayward," chanted the young man's choked voice, and I could not resist its lure. I crawled to where they stood and watched the winding tube-like tresses as the young man removed his spectacles, revealing fully his blemished eye. "Hayward," he laughed, licking his mouth with a soiled tongue. I set my lantern and book onto the ground as the mist that rose from the slab that was Obediah Carter's grave began to shape itself into a cruel and rapacious phantom, a ghost that sang my name. I raised my arms toward it, one of which was found by the smooth blade of Julia's antique razor.

Your Kiss of Corruption

I leaned against the cool wall of stone and listened to distant music. My brother had squandered his inheritance by purchasing the ancient Gothic church that was now our home and the show place of his vast collection of esoteric art and *objets d'art*. I had inherited father's magnificent library, and thus I spent my time alone, in my chilly chamber, reading and dreaming. The fortune that had been bequeathed to me was the money on which we lived; and it was also that which financed Christopher's lavish galas, the events that bored me but which I listlessly attended because I my brother decreed that it be so. It was at the last such affair that my brother had unveiled his latest acquisition, an ancient full-length mirror encased in a frame of white gold. Never before had such an unveiling been more successful; for the idiots who were his conceited friends lined up so as to admire themselves on the surface of polished glass. The sight of their uncouth cavorting, and the sound of their nonsensical shrieking, was too much for my nerves, and thus I walked out to the strange and venerable burying ground, to the queer and time-worn arched entrance of a buried mausoleum. Above its cavity of ingress was chiseled this curious inscription:

Mors Janua Vitae.

I leaned my brow against the cool rough stone of the neglected tomb and listened to the cry of night-birds. Quietly, I whispered the words of the inscription into the absolute darkness beyond the arched entrance. I felt the cold lips that kissed my neck; I felt them press against my ear and sigh the Latin epigraph. I could smell the bourbon on his breath.

"You're a naughty wretch, Agnes, to exile yourself from our

company. Come, let my friends adore your beauty; you look fetching in that tight dress, which clings to you like second skin. Come." His cool hand touched my arm.

"I'm in need of air. I'll join you anon." I looked up at the yellow moon and my flesh chilled at how macabre that sphere looked, casting its morbid light on the dismal place wherein we stood. Had the atmosphere grown cooler, or was it some psychic premonition of what was to come that caused my flesh to creep? When I finally turned to gaze into my brother's eyes, I saw within their luster a kind of craziness; and when his hands were suddenly pressing my arms against the cold surface of the mausoleum I suddenly panicked. "No," I told him.

"Be not afraid," he whispered. "I know you abhor the darkness. It's such a childish fear," he mocked. "Darkness is our friend. Here, let me lead you into this depth of blackness, and you'll find that you have naught to fear." I cried in pain at the tight hold of his hand around my wrist. "Come, Agnes, don't fight me."

"Let go of me, brother."

"Come, it's just a few steps down, and then you'll stand again on solid ground. We can lay together on one of the oblong tombs that hold the remains of some long forgotten sod. Come, follow me."

He had stepped into the shadow and was tugging my arm; yet still I resisted, and when I yanked my hand from him he tripped over his feet in trying to pull me to him. We both fell – I onto the cold hard ground, he down the rough-hewn steps into the place of darkness. Nervously, I clutched at the stiff dead grass and listened for his curses, but there was no sound, excepting the distant crying of a night-bird that pursued its prey. I looked up at the moon and winked at it, and I could feel its alchemy pour onto my eyes. It felt like a moment of magick, and I arose in lunar light like some dark goddess. "Rest in peace, my brother," I whispered, sighing my hot breath into the cavity of blackness. How strange that I could see that emanation of breath spill from me like some sentient thing and float into the deep darkness of the quiet tomb. What a sweet fragrance it had as it wafted from me and spilled into the hidden place.

I returned to the gaiety of my brother's party, and when a servant offered me a glass of dark red wine, I took it and drank. Passing the crowds, I smiled at the idiots who ignored me, who knew me merely as my brother's moody sibling. Sauntering past them, I went to the corner where stood the marvelous antique mirror. Sharing a secret smile with my reflection, I brought the glass of wine to my lips and let the warm liqueur trickle sweetly down my throat. Laughing, I hurled my glass to the floor and watched it shatter. I turned to grimace at those who stood nearest me, those frowning denizens of my brother's insipid world. They stood before me, like so many monsters of mediocrity, whispering as they watched me. I licked my lips and tasted a remnant of the delicious wine. Mouthing drunken mirth, I clutched at the tight fabric of my gown and ripped it apart, then tore my arms free and let the top portion of my gown fall around my waist, where it hung like some discarded skin. Motioning to a servant who stepped toward me with concern playing in his eyes, I demanded wine, and when he brought me another glass I turned to study my reflection in the mirror. I breathed heavily as I watched the rise and fall of my manumitted tits, and I laughed as I baptized them with a splash of rich red wine.

A commotion went through the crowd behind me, and I watched in the mirror their reflected horror as they fled the place in terror. One figure stood alone in the golden chandelier light. The doors leading outside had been left open by the mad crowd, and the night wind that rushed through those doors pushed the smell of blood and death through the room, to me. I shut my eyes to the macabre image in the mirror. I felt the cold lips that kissed my neck; I felt them press against my ear and breathe into that organ a soft exhalation that smelled of the fragrance that had slipped from my mouth when I had stood before the mausoleum and bade my brother peace. Turning, I faced the ungodly thing and touched a hand to where its head was split. Its face was sticky with coagulated blood, and I pressed the little bit of brain that peeped through where the skull had cracked after the figure's violent fall. A stream of blood spilled from where my finger had pierced into the dome, and as the thing bent to kiss my breast, it baptized my bosom with blood. I felt the carrion tongue that lapped the spill of wine that stained my flesh. The shattered face rose before my own, and although the maw that was its mouth moved, no exhalation floated from it. There was only the uttered lonesome gagging, a hungry sound. I bent to that mouth and kissed it, and

49

breathed my hot living air into it. The dry dead hand that wrapped around my wrist tugged as I was led out of the edifice, into night, toward the moonlight mausoleum where I would lie with kindred.

Yon Baleful God

How pale the sapphire of the central night,
Wherein the stars turn grey.

-Clark Ashton Smith

I sat within a moonlit glade on a summer's night. The air was very still, and the starlight over Sesqua Valley seemed sad and pale. I was staring into that melancholy light when, from out of woodland shadow, a figure limped toward me. I took in his lean disheveled form, the shock of unruly hair, the emaciated face. How odd that the moon's glow played strangely on one of his eyes. He knelt in front of me and bent his mouth to mine. The taste of his kiss was familiar. I pulled him to the ground and made love to his throat, his mouth – his chilly cheek. Lifting my head, I looked more closely at the pale dead eye that had replaced his socket's living orb.

"What's this?"

"It's something I had fashioned in Prague. Oh, Adam, I have found the lair of the forgotten god! I discovered the place where innocence was slaughtered in his name. I found the place where uncanny gems were offered to his mystery. I took one such gem and had it shaped so as to replace the eye that I have sacrificed in his name. There it is, snug in my socket, the jewel that he loved to look at, the surface of which caught his reflection in flickering torch light. His shadow became a living stain that adhered to the gemstone I had purloined. Look closely at that ornament, my love, and see the wonder that it adds unto me. Gaze deeply into its surface, Adam, and you will see him."

I touched the stiff and chilly flesh that was nearest to the artificial eye. I leaned nearer to that flesh and kissed it with my hot mouth. My lips touched the jewel's smooth surface. When I lifted my head and gazed steadfastly at that pale orb, I saw within it a swirling shadow that slowly took on form. I saw the visage that pierced that shadow with its majesty, that broke through and gazed at me with inhuman eyes. My lover raised his mouth to my ear and whispered one unholy name.

"Tsathoggua."

* * *

That night, in bed, he spoke of forgotten deities, gods formed in chaos beyond the known dimensions; things that pulsed in alien spaces between the stars. I listened, enthralled. We had spoken often of such things. I had shown him books and sculptures, bas-reliefs and tiaras on which were depicted the likenesses of unimaginable things. He wore himself out with talking that night. The pain in his injured leg began to throb. I held him in my arms and sang him to sleep. His head pressed against my chest, and the texture of the flesh near to the daemonic eye chilled me to my heart. That cold sensation slowed the pounding of my organ and seemed to seep into my veins, where it flowed toward my brain and blessed me with unholy vision. I squatted within a vaulted chamber. Strewn before me were the dry bones of offerings devoured long ago. In lethargy I sat and dreamed, recalling a time when I had known the succulent taste of sacrifice. Near to me was the dry husk of one long-dead offering, its skeletal hand stretched toward me. Within the palm of bone were pale gems that had been offered in obsequious veneration. I discerned upon their smooth surface my hoary reflection. I gazed for an eternity at the semblance of a forgotten god. And when at last I shut my weary eyes, I dreamt of sacrifice, of cindery human substance. And when I awakened it was to the scent of living flesh, which I but vaguely recalled. I gazed at the empty palm of bone, from which my gems had been pilfered. Sniffing air, I found a fragrance of mortal flesh and tangy blood. It brought to my senses a memory of sacrificial slaughter.

And then the scene melted and became dark. I lay within a shadowed chamber with my lover in my arms, his throat pressed against my mouth. I sucked at his salty flesh and bit into it. He moaned softly as I moved my tongue into the new wound. Outdoors, the night was haunted by the undulate song of numberless toads.

* * *

He awakened me before dawn and took my hand. Naked, we walked into woodland, to a ring of sacrificial stones. Legend told that the poet and sculpture William Davis Manly has chiseled the large rocks into the likenesses of things seen in disturbed dreaming, faces that called for blood and death. I had brought my lover to this place when first I lured him to Sesqua Valley and taught him our ways. He had been a dreamy boy, lonely and forsaken by those he loved and on whom he had depended. I nurtured his wounded psyche and taught him of the Old Ones who would not desert him. He did not disappoint me. Alone, he journeyed to the places outside the valley where he could find the arcane things. Now he had returned, to share with me the lore that had educated him.

Together we knelt within the ring of stones, and he whispered to me the unwholesome name. "Tsathoggua. I can see him, waiting patiently for when the stars come right and he will grow strong and liberated. Ah, how he hungers for cosmic freedom, to seep toward starlight and find his home. But he is weak – only sacrifice will make him strong. Let us assist him, Adam. Look, this discarded stone here, it's heavy and will do the trick. Hold it high above my head as I lay down my life for the thing that begs for veneration. Let us offer him a new sacrifice, my love."

I took the heavy stone from his hands as he reclined upon the ground. His smile was a beautiful thing. I took in his handsome face and then smashed that beloved visage with the weighty rock. Sighing, I took from the remains of his pulp the filthy gem that had usurped a living eye. I gazed hard at the shadow within its pale surface and saw the bestial face that smiled.

Time of Twilight

(For Quentin Crisp)

The small apartment smelled of age. A single window allowed a partial view of a city bathed in mellow late afternoon sunlight. I went to that window and watched the setting sun as the elderly man removed his velvet hat and jacket, his scarf of white silk, his battered cloth shoes. I turned and watched as he stopped before a mirror so as to reapply lipstick to his painted face. He wore his withered beauty well. "This is a wonderful rouge," he told me, "moist and creamy, and the color stays vibrant for hours. Would you care to try it?"

I laughed. "No thank you."

"Ah, well; your lips wear youth's beauty, but at my age I need assistance. Not that I wish to look young. I've had my sunlit years of golden youth. I'm rather glad to be rid of them. The charm of old age is that one may overact appallingly. One is free of youthful vanity."

"Oscar Wilde would disagree. What did he once write, that the tragedy of old age is that one is young?"

He tossed to me a splenetic frown. "He never lived to see fifty. I've never been in agreement with Mr. Wilde. I doubt that he believed half the things he so cleverly uttered. He was performing for an audience that would eventually destroy him, poor sod. He expired because society turned its back to him. I prefer honest rebels, which is why I frequent the youthful society at the club where I encountered you. I see there such honest wildness, an anarchy that I can believe in."

"And were you a wild young thing?"

"I was a rebel, absolutely. In my day it was a scandal for a woman to wear crimson nail varnish, unless she was a punk. For a man to do likewise..." He saw his past in daydream, and then swept the memory away. "I had to pay a price, naturally. All wonderful things demand sacrifice." Joining me at the window, he studied my face in dying light. "You are quite lovely, dear boy. How I adore you young men who dress in black. It's my favorite shade, is black. Looks very good on you, with your wild hair and wounded eyes. At times I behold such awesome beauty and momentarily mind that I'm so aged." He stood back some so as to admire my figure. "Now, what does it say on your tight shirt? I can't quite make it out."

"Thanatos."

"How grim. Perhaps it is the name of your favorite band?"

"It's my profession."

Beautifully, he smiled. "Ah! I *thought* I recognized you when I saw you gazing at me through that cloud of cigarette smoke. Well, dear me. The oldest profession in the world – next to whoredom, of course. How delightful. You've come at last in answer to mumbled prayer. God knows how often I've called to you, kneeling in this squalid den. I always knew that you would be shockingly beautiful."

I sighed. "Mortals usually fear and loathe me. Rarely have I been so adored. You've touched me, and in gratitude I shall bestow upon you my most tender kiss."

He gazed beyond me into darkening heaven. "Will it be a kiss of oblivion? I couldn't stand any kind of eternity. Will you grant me shadow absolute?"

"Certainly."

His eyes twinkled. "Joyous day! I am your own." He knelt before me, and his lovely eyes shimmered like a pair of happy stars. I fell to my knees beside him and let my semblance of flesh slip from me. Rapturously, he gasped. I brushed his mauve hair with hands of bone. His liquid eyes were bright with tears. Oh, those eyes! Lovelier than the prettiest of stars. Leaning to me, he kissed my grin. I caught him as he gasped, and held him close. I felt the fleeting tremors of his heart. Raising to me his weary face, he gazed at me with those alchemical eyes. Yes, I would grant him eternal darkness, but I could not surrender his awesome eyes. I plucked them from his nodding head and thrust them into gathering twilight. They sailed beyond the moon, burning with the beauty of his fading soul. Sighing, I wound myself around him, ushering him into the shadow of my eternal embrace.

These Deities of Rarest Air

A Prose-Poem Sequence

I.

I press my weakened knee upon the ground and cry the call, for I would know your shadow on my brow, blossoming, and sense the arcane things endow my mundane mind with ceremonial task, rich ritual, the pleasures of daemonic design. I cry for they who come to press mouths upon my eyes, beneath which they sink so as to suck my burning brain from out its dungeon, my smooth skull. Allow me to let loose this essence of mortality that welds me to this world, this earth; then let me crawl into some cosmic place where weakened limbs are démodé, where pangs of fleshy pain are but a jest bequeathed by mirthless gods. I will dance as I eschew oxygen for that other element.

Yet I, still pressed upon this solid ground, cannot ascend unto yon floating clouds, and my one task is to claw into the mud in which I write your immemorial name, the name that once more I call to those dark clouds with mouth that sucks in the current of this paltry age. I ache to suck a rarer clime, where I can drift as acolyte of smoke among the nightmares of an alien dimension, where earth and its happy doom is but a memory that makes me chuckle into the void – the endless abyss in the gulf of night where I would waft with chilly cosmic tempest that is the exhalation from your maw, that mouth with which you speak my mortal name and claim me as your own.

II.

I cannot see the flowers at my feet, the emblems of remembrance at my tomb, for smoke and shadow cloud what once were eyes; but I can sense the soft bouquet of rose and smell the wilted lily's rank decay. I drift through weightless air on buoyant feet until I find again the gems that were your eyes, jewels that burn with self-substantial fire, ignition that pronounces you a god, embedded in your basalt eidolon. I fall to shattered knee on polished floor of one posthumous place, a floor that is littered by the remembrance of flowers from your once-living devotee. She could not last forever. Had I lips I would moan your name as dark psalm, the name I almost seem to recollect, that once I whispered in the realm of life. Although we both are dead, dread lord, I heard your uncanny call in termination's dusk, and from my final slumber I awakened, to rise from rotted wood and strata of earth, to you and to a memory of life. I thought in death to become a thing of air, lifted from the elements of time; but I am still a creature of debris, transformed into neglected dust and mud. Like you, I am forgotten and bereft. Like you, I find no solace in the worm. To you I would exhale liturgical utterance and clasp my hands in unholy solitude. Yet I am but a puppet of the grave, animated by your alchemy, and all that I can offer you, dread lord, is veneration of a hollow heart, and veneration from a mouth of filth that falls more apart with each impotent whimper, until I am returned to my filthy bed, where I will worship you if I am able, wrapped with worms.

III.

I breathe into the fitful air as the alchemy of consumption has begun, as all my physicality wastes away, as I become an element of air until I am an exhalation lifting to the skies, a vapor in a draft of wind. As I evaporate into the clouds, like some meditation on mortality, I take on the aspect of a whispered word that may, by chance, be nothing but a name, a name that one may whisper in a prayer to some strange thing beyond sane dimension, a power pulsing in-between the stars into which my essence is inhaled. I filter through the clouds now wet with rain, like some forgotten word once writ on water, forgotten by the faces far below that open mouths so as to drink the downpour, mouths that cannot remember me with speaking. And thus I drift in anonymous void, like some sad ghost that has lost its earthly hold, and fly toward the thing that, pulsing, sucks me into nothingness divine. And there I am surrounded by rare sparks, ignition that issues from a flaming throne, where chaos chatters idiotically, and the Strange Dark One offers me a pipe, which taking I press to malformed mouth, so as to join the disturbance that makes the dark air tremble, the psalm of sound that will go on and on, beyond the death of time.

IV.

We climb the haunted hill to its highest tip, to one place where memory is entombed beneath the clouds, those clouds that seem to form fantastic beings who watch our secret play. The thing reclines upon the tabletop tomb where once it ate, where once it had been eaten, long ago. Its hollow bones are blanched by burning sun. We remove the dust of time from off the bones with our unhallowed tongues, the dust that is not bitter to the taste; and we remember, vaguely, the flavor of sweet soft flesh, partaken beneath the silent watchful clouds, the flesh on which we dined so long ago, devoured in remembrance of our gods. The book of ritual is clasped in hand of bone, the book he held at time of sacrifice. You take it from his frail fossilized hand as I move my lips to that cavity that was his mouth and housed the tongue that moved with ours in praise to they who dwell above us in the clouds. You take the book of ritual in hand and speak the words that turn the white sun red, as the bones beneath me crumble into dust, as I recline upon the tabletop slate and turn to gaze into daemonic sky as your sweet mouths clamp onto my tissue and pay homage to our gods

V.

An arsenical moon, disrobed of clouds, hangs in suicidal sky, and I drink that moon like laudanum and sprinkle into its nectar crushed pearls of starlight. I take that horned moon and slit the wrist of heaven, and smell the seepage of cosmic blood that taints the scent of night. I conjure forth the wind that soughs through dancing trees and sounds like the rustling of purple satin curtains that hide my antics from the dreary crowd. I seep between those curtains and stalk the night in memory of you, Mateo, beneath that vaulted tomb, the sky. I take your spectral hand, my lovely lad, and kiss it with pale lips on which passion has cooled but that remember still your taste. I pray to you, my deity of love, and dance with memory in the lost places one can only find in dream. Sing to me, Mateo, my deity of sorrow, so that I may follow your voice through mortal air, unto a place of ghosts that know nothing of unwanted passion.

VI.

I step into the subterranean place and breathe chthonic air that still contains a memory of that which oozed from your infernal prehistoric lungs. I sense the recollection of your home, that darker planet deep in cosmic void, unadorned by glow of moon or star, from which you fell through non-dimensional space and time to sleepy mud beneath our ancient hill. I find it here, upon your obsidian dais, among the jewels that have never known the light of dawn, and marvel at the expert articulation that may be uttered by an artifact. I shine my torch onto your representation, and sense that you recoil from the touch of ersatz illumination that filters artificially through darkness. I kill the light and see you with my senses, as the gems that are my eyes adjust to darkness, wherein I see things in a different fashion, as I suck in air that reeks of your bequeathed diseases; and as I peer into the air of this dimension, the place begins to shape itself anew, until I understand that I now stand within the ebon caverns of N'Kai, in which I bow my altered form, no longer human now but serpentine, and weep your praises with my dying breath.

VII.

How queer, these things that one can sense in darkness. It is not imagination; it is not, I fear, even madness; and memory, or its tatters, is a damnation that threatens to grow unambiguous. I recall the scent of morning, mostly sweet and succulent like meadow dew, yet tainted slightly by an indistinct debauch. I remember my first sight of blurry dawn as weighty lids arose, meekly and minutely. There is recollection of muted yet excited voices, of the faces of men that take on solid outline as the light that spills in through high windows caught the features of these fellows. I did not deign to open my eyes too widely, unused as they were to earthly light, nor did I shift as one of the mortals bent over me with a chilly apparatus, one part of which he placed against my chest as its other end was fastened to his ear. How distasteful it was, to be touched and violated; but my limbs proved stiff and heavy, and would not move in protest beneath mortal hands; nor could I split my mouth in protest as a needle was injected yet again into my heart, as something from within that implement flowed through me, something smooth and cool and sinister. Rough mortal hands clutched at me, and I was lifted from the surface on which I reclined, carried some little distance and then dropped into an uncouth pit from which I could discern the fragrance of freshly violated earth. Words, muttered in discouragement and anger, faded, and I sensed that I had been abandoned in the lonesome place.

The blur of hateful day grew more intense as it blazed from the high wide windows, and the ghouls who were my guardians did not return. More and more, the burning liquid that had been injected into my heart pumped through my veins, and thus I was invigorated. With a sense of doubtful liberation I clutched at the walls of my pit and pushed hands into its sediment, where I found enough of a hold so that I could pull myself onto my knees. My eyes now fully functioned, and with them I scrutinized the floor of earth around me and its other crude pits, some of which were hideously inhabited. There were tables and their implausible instruments, the sight of which brought nagging memory to mind. Of a place where I had labored in stealth, in some secret chamber, combining powders and fluids as I uttered incantations from the Aklo tablets. I saw within my mind's depths the beings of another realm that had answered my incantations, creatures that were not angelic. These fiends pushed against my moving mouth and stole my mortal exhalation until sensation expired and sentient darkness wove around and through me. Time transformed, and soon I smelled the muted light of new dawn; and lifting my face to that soft light I experienced renewed strength, and crawled out of the shallow indentation into which the ghouls had tossed me. Creeping to a vast wooden vat that squatted on naked earth, I curled my fingers around its rim so as to regain threatened balance; and as I clutched that rim I studied the unnatural blanched pastiness of my hands, soiled as they had been by earth's debris. I steadied on painful knees and bent over the vat's wooden rim. I watched the white reflection of the ghastly thing I had become as it wavered in the vat's liquid, wavered because my shuddering was shaking the wooden tub. I shook because I was a thing that should not – or should no longer – exist. Oh, bleached and bony countenance, what horror you portend, what breach of sanity; for I was a madness out of time, disrupted in my final rest by the fluid that had been injected into my diseased heart. My mouth then found its voice, and I whimpered at my fate.

Uneasily, I stood. Ungainly, I stalked to a door and shook it from its hinges, then tramped upon it as it crashed onto the ground. Unnaturally, I breathed, and the sound of that exhalation was conjoined with a groan of unutterable misery. I walked until the yellow sky darkened and a bloated moon appeared, a fungal chimera deep within an abyss of night. I walked instinctively, until I found the plot from which I had been robbed. The ground of my grave had been smoothed, its desecration concealed. I tried to speak the name that had been etched onto my tombstone, but naught slipped from my mouth except a gag of woe. When I dropped onto the ground, my fingers found their way homeward into the earth. The smell of displaced sod began to soothe me, and as I worked I tried to sing a memory of magick that was one portion of the Aklo formulae with which, in other existence, I communed with deities of rarest air. And the sound of my strangled voice lifted to the fungal moon, which was soon camouflaged by shapes that were not clouds, fiends that fell to me. They wove around and through me as I reclined within my new-made pit, as I pulled the displaced silt over me, until it covered me completely.

VIII.

Looking inward, she saw naught but phantoms – fiends that, churning, laced her heart with doom. She did not mind that this was so; for she had wearied of humanity and its unhappy world, where in delusion its inhabitants danced and warbled of nothing beneath their expiring sun. She loathed them and their senseless frolic, and hated the way their sunlit faces condemned her malcontent. They could never comprehend her, and thus she felt kinship with fiends alone, those things of smoke and madness that churned around her brain and sank into her heart, where they taught that organ deadlier palpitation. And thus she secreted herself in one lonesome place, a place of death where happy mortals were disinclined to play; and there she danced with vines of willow trees and sang to startled bats, and answered the baying that drifted to her on the midnight wind, the howling of some unearthly thing that hungered for blood and tears. She danced, accompanied by her shadowed fiends, those comrades that melted into her heart and taught it deceleration, an alien palpitation that pulsed inside her throat and lifted to the back of her eyes, her eyes to which were revealed an obscure realm where dreams festered and became merrily diseased.

She floated on daemoniac tempest which lifted her to a high wall, on which she balanced beneath a foggy violet welkin; and through mists that were the miasmal pants of devils she watched one star, the name of which she might once have known but had forgotten, and thus she could not call to it. Yet still its dim refraction bent the air above her so that shadows, falling, took her hands and guided her along the wall, until they reached a place where a sluggish river wound its lethargic way. Her shadows held her as she jumped from off the wall and landed near the bridge that crossed the river, could cross so as to journey to the distant paddock beneath a violet heaven, and to the antediluvian tower of blanched stone that tilted over that eerie meadow. She skipped across the bridge and danced toward the tower, which rose from earth like some prehistoric relic of bone; and she marveled at how that tower shimmered beneath the violet heaven, as if its substance drank the illumination that leaked from the daemon-star. She smiled and kissed the tower's rock, and entered the arched threshold that led within the edifice, to circular steps that rose toward violet heaven and its single star. She climbed to the upper reaches and found one large and lonely window, through which she leaned toward chill infinity; and as she scanned the sky her inner-fiends ceased their churning and spilled from out her eyes, leaking into the violet abyss above her, toward the daemon-star, that sphere from which there fell one silver beam that served as path into the gulf of night. And on that path she stepped, dancing toward the star that diffused with the shadows of her fiends, in whose quiet conclave she would find rare dreams and darkness eternal.

IX.

Where can I learn the doctrine of the mask? I seem to sense it in voltage of the sky, where fissures of fire split the gulf of night and almost spell your name. I watch the electric show as those streams of lightning fall toward the expanse of water into which I wade, the lightning that flashes so as to reveal your black visage there, where once a moon arose. Innsmouth, with her unnumbered crimes, sleeps behind me. I walk among the antique wooden buoys, those markers on which curious hand-carved faces watch my stride. The green illumination of your eyes is reflected on the water through which I amble, the water that tingles with the kiss of your electric show. Peering into the depths, I see the other eyes of deep things far below, and I see the mouths below those eyes that would part and drag me under with their siren song. Have you devoured the moon, that mistress of the tides? Your black façade is like a magnet to my blood, and I pulled deeper there, into the depths, where your cruel visage is reflected. It drifts to me, on the water, your mask of manifestation; and I would lift it to me, but the liquid of which it is composed spills through my fingers. How can I don the doctrine of your mask and be your child? That is my deepest dream. Perhaps if I sink beneath the surface, just below your veneer of mockery, I can then lift upward, out of water, with your features melted into mine own. But that is a mistake; for as I sink beneath the surface, I hear at last the liquid song of they who hunger for my mortal soul. Their clamor rises, claiming me as a whirlpool of inhuman echo. And you, above, smile and scorn, at the center of the liquid vortex, adored by the chiseled faces of the antique buoys.

X.

I thought to adore you, beast of the godless valley, and sing your psalms to haunted shadow – a haunting sound. I am intoxicated by your scent, the cloying sweetness that is a manifestation of this realm, a fragrance that is embedded in your hair, your hands, your mouth. Oh, the hunger you inspire, the rush of blood and quake of bones. Yet you allow me to worship from a distance only, after your initial seduction; and your indifference serves to flame my need, so that I fall onto my knees among the haunted shadow and sink my fingers into the soil that shares your scent. I lift that mud and wash it over my visage, and wear it as a mask of fragrant filth; and that is when you kneel before me, and smile with silver eyes as you whisper secrets to the hungry sky, the sky that clouds with shapes that adore you more than I. And as those airy outlines in the sky sing your psalms with unsubstantial maws, your aromatic hands work the soil of my mask, and it is strange, to be so molded and malformed. I do not mind, for when you grace me with the nearness of your perfumed face, I see what I have become there, on the surface of your silver eyes; and I know that, now adopted by the vale, I shall dwell with you forever.

XI.

"To our porphyry tombs, dear Robbie, and to the worm!" We sat in Oscar's enchanting garden, beneath an autumn moon, and I tapped my glass of absinthe to his.

"To love – and to its loss," I countered, and he momentarily frowned, then shrugged and drank the elixir.

"Love is often a tomb in which the heart is trapped," he offered, "gnawed by that foul worm, passion. I am happy to be aged, to have put all of that nonsense behind me. How joyous, to peep at that far moon and not have to sigh for romance. What happiness, to feel in one's heart the chilliness of that supernal sphere of dust and to share in her frigidity, in this eleventh hour of my mortality."

"So you say." He frowned and squinted suspiciously. I smiled. "Yet you still adore the form of youth that drove you to insanity in former days. Or so your recent acquisition would suggest; for there he stands, among the mauve and purple hyacinth, a dark phantom of male perfection."

Oscar did not deign to turn and study the object of which I spoke. Rather, setting down his glass, he opened his cigarette case and took up an opium-tainted cylinder of shredded tobacco. I refused when he offered me to select my own. "Yes, he stands there as those lovely flowers dance in this mild autumn zephyr. His figure is sublime – but you have failed to notice his most singular feature."

"Have I?" Moving out of my chair, glass in hand, I walked down the little path that took me to the spot where the figure had been planted. I assumed it was made of smooth and polished wood that had been stained so as to give it its hue of utter blackness. I guessed it to be five feet in height, and the taut perfection of its figure made clear that its model had been a superb Adonis of an athletic kind. "It is of Greek or African origin," I told my host. "Its pose is certainly interesting – it seems a haughty stance, and the one uplifted arm rather demands the adoration of one's mouth, commanding to be kissed. How peculiar that it was left unfinished."

My back was to Oscar, and so I could not see if he would rise to join me. I heard his exhalation and smelled the perfumed smoke that drifted to me on the wind. "Why do you assume it is unfinished?"

I rotated and returned to where he sat. "Because you have always had an obsession for the face of perfect handsomeness – and there is no visage on that effigy of wood. There is naught but a smooth and perfect blankness, a void of features."

"Could not such a void prove symbolic?"

Quietly, I laughed. "Of what?"

"Did his facelessness not suggest anything to you, dear Robbie?" Snuffing out his cigarette, he rose and wandered to the figure. "Do you not notice how there is an aspect of listening in his haughty tilt of head, as if the void where his face should be is an audient thing that awaits our whispered veneration? And did you not notice the little points of light that play upon his void, almost indiscernible but fathomed nonetheless? When one studies them carefully, one can see that they are reflections of those gathered stars, just there, in the gulf of night – that peculiar pattern of cosmic points that hang so suggestively in night's abyss."

"What nonsense you talk, Oscar." And then the alcohol got to me, and triggered a dull ache within the fissure in my skull. Silently, my friend observed me, and then he sallied to me and placed his white gloved hand against my forehead. He loved to touch the place of abnormal absence just beneath my face.

"It feels more pronounced, this split in your frail skull – extending like a fissure on some house of Usher."

"Do take your mitten away, old thing. You needn't analyze my infirmity – I can feel its expansion, from the roof of my dome to the cellar of my soul; for it is more than a physical cleft, and like poor Roderick I can hear its division in my pit of psyche. In time it will grow so wide that my brain will wash its fluid to my eyes, and in that vision I will behold my death. So fill your glass again, my friend, and let us toast our perishability."

"Enough. Death is wonderful as a poetic toy – but its reality is too dull for words. Let us not speak of terminations – for that is not dead which may linger for an eternity, beneath the earth, the sea, or deep within some unknown gulf of night. No, do not frown on me with your dark suspicious eyes. I do not jest, nor am I a drunken sphinx with riddles to unravel. You know that I returned some little time ago from Côte d'Ivoire, from which I appropriated yon mythic eidolon. I learned of it in *Al Azif,* a kaleidoscope of allegorical poetry, the author of which has been deemed 'mad' by undiscerning minds. I ascertained where I would find the Faceless Eikon, of which I began to dream. To absorb *Al Azif* is to realize dreams such as one has never known. And in those visions of this nameless Eikon I saw that it, too, dreamt – of me! Our dreaming *coalesced,* hideously, and in those visions I heard the song that was chanted to the Faceless Eikon, its psalms of adoration that were mouthed by lesser deities of strangest air. The language of that ritual clings to my brain with such intensity that I feel my skull, like yours, must split. In one queer dream I danced before the Eikon, and from above there issued a panorama of electric streams that, flashing brightly, revealed the forms of faces that blossomed and withered on the surface where the Eikon wore no countenance – and among those fleeting phizogs, momentarily, I beheld your own."

"*Al Azif* – such a queer sound, those words, especially as spoken on your tongue; for you say them as only a poet can, endowing them with potency of language."

"*Azif* designates a peculiar sound associated with nocturnal insects, or what might be mistaken as insects, that is a local legend in the land where the mad Arab penned his lines and diagrams. Perhaps it is a drone that one can only hear in dream – and yet, perhaps, as our reality influences what we dream, perhaps the devils that dream of us influence our existence."

"You've lost me, entirely, old thing."

He shrugged. "Old I am. But there are others, great old things that dream in rare dimension; and in their dreams they smell our mortal blood, that rare elixir that is especially to this globe. They are enticed, by smell of blood and the repast of which it promises. And so they seek us out, in our dreaming and our lunacy, manifesting themselves in secret ceremony and fantastic art. They motivated some savage to sculpt that esoteric Eikon from some trunk of tree." He looked at me so oddly. "They inspired me to summon you here tonight, so that I may spill into your ear the language of their alchemy."

"Have you ever enunciated this foreign language?"

"In dream alone."

"And how we speak in dream can be so peculiar. Things happen in a nap, with our eyelids closed, that we think consume a day, yet are the matter of mere seconds. How fanciful earthly time can be, in realm of slumber."

"Then let us dream while wide-awake," Oscar sighed as he took me in his arms. I stood very still as he pressed his lips against my ear, into which he uttered alien lexis. I heard that utterance coil around my brain, and then it seemed to spill from out the fissure in my skull, into the upper aether; and from that height I heard the language spoken by other tongues, as a song of infernal buzzing, and between the phrases I heard the spoken name of "Nyarlathotep," a name that shook the firmament. And I saw a cloud assemble in the heavens, black and nebulous, shifting its form until it resembled the wooden statue of my friend. It billowed to me from the air, surrounded by its devils, they who buzzed his name in adoration. And then the droning horde fell to me and melted through my face. They found the fissure in my cranium and entered in, and I clasped my hands to ears in an attempt to stop their whirring pulsation. I shut my eyes so as to block the phantom in the sky and its supernal mockery – but this was a mistake, for suddenly my identity clouded, became doubtful. Was I standing in the garden of my poetic friend, or was I whirling inside my skull with a daemon horde to which I had conjoined? Why did I *remember* impossible things, alien and incredible scenes beneath the combustion of violet suns, cyclopean cylinders of rotting stone that tilted over fungous vegetation?

Another devil spoke the majestic name, a rapacious lunatic who usurped my place in infamy. Oscar pushed me from the hand that the fluctuating form of Nyarlathotep was offering me, and as I toppled onto his garden he bent to that cosmic hand and licked it; and then he howled, but only once, for as he wailed his features melted from him, and without his mouth he could no longer utter sound. I watched him fall next to me, into his hyacinths, as his body boiled and burned and blackened; and then at last he extinguished, a black and faceless thing, to which I crawled, and over which I wept.

XII.

I crept like a frightened girl on silver-sandaled feet beneath an arc of moonlight, toward the House of Shadows. The street of sorrow on which I tiptoed was as hard as cold reality – I was eager to be off it; and so I rushed to the porch when I beheld it, and hopped onto its first step with a relish of satisfaction. But my pleasure was short-lived, for as I skipped up the wooden steps I encountered a splinter that drove into my heel. Thus wounded, I limped through the threshold, into the edifice. The hallway was very dark, except for sad phosphorescent faces that floated, here and there, along the low ceiling and provided the single source of light. I stopped to rest my stinging foot and leaned against a tall grandfather clock, resting my head against its mirrored door and listening to its pulse; and as I rested I watched the blanched face that, floating to the clock, kissed its own reflection on the polished glass. The ticking from behind that glass extinguished and time became extinct; but then I heard another rhythm that sounded from behind one nearest door. Stepping to that door, I turned its knob and entered into a spacious chamber that vibrated with music that was performed by a band of mechanical grotesques. Masked gigolos moved in solitary dance around a small fountain that gurgled in the middle of the room. I laughed at their clumsy movement, and at the sound of my derision one figured jerked toward me; and as it studied me in the chamber's artificial light I could see that its whorish limbs were made of wood, smooth and white. Reaching out, I removed its pallid mask so as to reveal the puppet countenance, a physiognomy so smooth and fine and handsome that I could not resist tilting to it and pressing my lips to its unyielding mouth. Lifting the pallid mask above me, I marveled at its beguiling velvetiness, and I could not resist lowering it onto my face and pressing it against my tingling flesh, to which it sensuously adhered. The handsome puppet took my hands and waltzed me to the fountain in the middle of the room, and I laughed merrily until I looked down into the water; for beneath that liquid surface I saw a bloated thing that I recognized as a boy I once had loved then tossed aside. He had been an elf of bewitching beauty, but addiction and ennui had debauched his loveliness and made him dull. I met him one last time on a bridge over a slow-moving river, where I whispered in moonlight that our love affair was over. Turning away from him, I whistled at the moon; but soon I heard a splashing sound. And looking down I saw a white sphere floating beneath the river water, and I knew that it was the submerged and lifeless face of my discarded lover. It bobbed once out of the water, so that his dark liquid eyes gazed at me one last time; and then the current pulled him down and out of view.

A wooden mouth pressed against my hair, and then my ear, and heaved in an artificial voice my lover's name; and yet I could not turn my eyes away from the phantom image in the fountain, and so I saw the dead bloated face arise and open its mouth, from which a stream of slime escaped. And I became furious; for I had escaped into the House of Shadows so as to escape sordid reality, yet here it was before me, risen as a swollen corpse that hungered for my kiss. I backed away from the cruel fountain and pushed the handsome dummy from me, and then I rushed to the doorway and fled the monstrous chamber. I ran, up carpeted stairs, into an upper region where I encountered a soft golden radiance that was like nothing known in harsh actuality. I sighed to that happy light and followed it into another room that was furnished with exquisite antiques. Smiling, I approached one upright mirror and winked at my image that was cased within the arch of golden filigree into which the mirror had been fitted. Foolishly, I began to caper before my double, wincing only slightly at the recurring throb of pain in my wounded heel when it struck too haughtily the floor. Yet I could not dance for long, because I grew so easily exhausted; and this perplexed me until I peered again into the pool of glass and saw my withered eidolon. How could the aged, decrepit creature in that mirror be me, with those bags below its rheumy eyes, its sagging flesh and scarecrow hair? I could not comprehend it.

And then my reflection did not dwell alone; and I sensed the form beside me, no longer a drowned and bloated husk of tiresome flesh, but a chilly solid reality that touched its hands to my hair. I watched in the mirror as his mouth kissed my hair, my throat, my breast. He lowered to his knees and kissed my foot, at which his fingers worked until, smoothly, he plucked the sharp sliver of wood from my heel. And then he rose before me one last time, the boy I had once adored and ruthlessly debauched, and a lovely little smile played on his lips, and he touched those lips to mine as he pushed the sharp, sharp splinter through my chest, into my heart.

XIII.

I disengage from legion and swim through black clouds to where the woman hangs, the crone who adored me with magick and mayhem before her filthy murder. She dangles, now, from length of hempen rope, as below her, in semi-circle, bay the green-eyed ghouls who were her pack. I used to hear her croon to them, in my spaces between the stars, and watched her share in their ghastly repast. I saw her kiss their eyes, those moonlit eyes that were of a similar shade to her green orbs. I float before them now, her wide and lifeless eyes, and kiss them with my devil breath, an exhalation to which her dead mouth lifts; and as her lips begin to curl with reanimation, the fire from my eyes cinders the rope on which she hangs. From some distant place behind me the scene is ruptured by a flash of false light, an element that I do not understand. No matter; the fire from my eyes has flayed the hempen rope from which she hangs, and thus she sallies from the gallows, to the ground and they who reach to catch her. I drift to her as cloud of daemon-smoke, and I melt into her flesh and find new compartment in her heart, which beats to the rhythm of my enchantment. For there are times when we insubstantial freaks of alien dimension long to dwell within a mortal form, and we have found the easiest to reanimate are they who hang from gallows, or from isolated limbs in hidden forests, or from suicidal rafters in dreamer's attic. And thus we slip through elements beyond mortal imagination, to blend our spectres with this corporeal clime, and find the dead eyes of criminals and suicides, of they accused of witchcraft and other petty sins; and we evoke our reflected essence on those eyes until they blink and water with our alchemy, with life-in-death; and thus we teach stiff limbs to walk the earth again, to dance beneath the ghastly moon, as she dances now among her brood of ghouls.

The noisome pack arises so as to lick her gnarled hands and lift paws with which to soothe her broken neck. They do not seem to comprehend that it is another being that peers at them with her wild eyes. When at last I speak, it is with her harsh voice; and I lift her gnarled hands so as to make esoteric signals to the moon and bend the element of air. I have not forgotten that queer electric flash that rudely infiltrated the place earlier, and I am aware of the semi-human eyes that observe us from some hidden place, and I cackle as I use my alchemy so as to smooth and heal the hag's broken neck. I raise her reanimated eyes to the gallows on which she was murdered, and I spit my daemon fire to that gibbet and then dance with my ghouls as it is reduced to cinders. How delicious it was, to have a material body of mortal flesh, to no longer be a thing of daemonic aether, and to *feel* upon my newly-inhabited form those aspects of this physical plane, the heat of flames with which the gallows had been destroyed, the chilly expulsion of canine breath from the mouths of my ghouls as they licked me, the taste of carnage on those fiendish mouths as my pack kissed me. I rubbed my desiccated hands over my arms and pinched so as to feel the bone beneath. I sensed the world with mortal eyes and worked the brain within its cranium; and from that brain I culled the wise woman's esoteric knowledge, her craft, with which she had been able to evoke storms and make herself invisible. It was this latter art that most intrigued me, and so I shut my eyes and spoke her remembered spell, and my ghouls bayed when I vanished from their view. With invisibility came another aspect, an enhancement of being one with earthly elements; and so I conjoined to rising gale and floated to the hidden place, wherein I found the one who was concealed.

I spoke, and he rose from hiding and watched as I regained my solid form. I learned from dipping into his psyche that he was an artist of rare talent, and that the mechanical instrument that he wore around his neck was that with which he caught images with a form of modern alchemy. It was the instrument that had produced the rude flash of light that had earlier annoyed me. But more important than any of this were those aspects of his nature that he did not fully comprehend – his deep disturbance by the sight of my ghouls, and the longing that my pack aroused within some secret chamber of his soul. I lifted my withered hand so as to stroke his face, the face on which I saw heredity's stamp that shewed me what he was, a foundling that, with time, was stepping into genetic mutation of flesh and psyche. I would not explain this to him – he would realize all anon. I would give him but a taste of what in fact he was, what in time he would fully become. Tilting to him, I gave him her kiss, the brush of lips that she reserved for her especial brood. I kissed him as my pack raised their jade eyes (so like his own) and bayed to yellow moon. And I laughed as he, not understanding why, lifted his head to that lunatic satellite and bayed also.

XIV.

The party was not his kind of thing, but it was given by his friend and collaborator that All Hallow's Eve, and so Elias Koffen felt the need to attend, if only for a little while. The party's absurd theme – everyone had to dress as a character from a Vincent Price film – at first seemed absolutely puerile; but then he realized that he could take advantage of this theme to dress as a character from his favorite author, Poe. He paid an actress friend, who also had a private business as a seamstress, a small fortune to create a robe that was identical to that worn by Price in his beguiling role as The Red Death; and he had decided to wear crimson greasepaint over his face rather than a mask. He found, in a costume shop, an excellent pair of red velvet gloves that would be the perfect final touch. And so he sauntered into the party at 10.33 p.m., and frowned at the array of unimaginative costumes – the one exception being a deliciously masculine woman who looked exactly as Price in his role of Roderick Usher. He danced with her for a little while; but she was obviously intoxicated, and people who drank bored him, so he made his escape to his friend's small office and its excellent library of weird fiction. He glanced with subdued envy at the titles of those books his friend had written on his own: *The Delver Underneath*, by Ephraim Kant, *In the Valley of Shoggoth*, by Ephraim Kant, and so on; for solo production had been a trick that Elias had never mastered, and his one collection of stories written on his own, *The Feaster from Afar and Others*, had yet to find an interested publisher. He had had some few copies published at his own expense, bound in white vellum with title stamped in red, and he reached for the copy he had presented to his friend and cohort. He opened the book to that tale he considered his best, "The Mask of Outer Madness," and began to read aloud its opening paragraph:

> "During the entire dull day, as he lay within a pile of autumn leaves tinted gold, he had scanned the low oppressive cloud that seethed above him in the dark sky and imagined that it formed a daemon of amorphous dimension. He watched that monstrous cloud as the last remnant of daylight expired, and then he lifted out of leaves and proceeded on his way to the haunted church whose black steeple had been destroyed in last month's thunderstorm. At his first glimpse of it he suffered a pervasive gloom that saturated his soul with depression, for the bleak edifice seemed a personal comment on his wretched state of loneliness."

And then, within the quiet of the room that knew only his whispered language, Elias heard another soft voice continue to speak the opening paragraph of his tale.

> "And so he staggered, past the few white trunks of withered trees, with unearthly misery churning his little soul, as the mist of the moist ground rose to mask the building before him in a mauve haze that, as he breathed it in, seemed the very aether of damnation."

He was so startled that he almost dropped the book, and this reaction caused a low, blithe voice to laugh. He turned and whispered "Juliana," and at the name the beautiful woman genuflected, revealing a peek of the taut black breasts beneath the gown that replicated Hazel Court's costume in her final scene. Elias marveled at the beauty of the necklace of white gold around the black woman's throat, at the upside-down cross of darker gold just above the bosom. She did not wear a veil-like headpiece as the actress had in the film, but rather let her abundance of rich red hair fall down past her shoulders, reaching to the small of her back. When she stood erect and gazed at him, the writer saw that her jade eyes were flecked with gold.

"I've startled you," she sighed.

"In more ways than one," he responded. "Were you reading behind my back?"

"Not at all. I am intimate with your work." She held out a hand. "Marceline Rableau." He took her hand and kissed it, then repeated the name in a quiet voice as he tried to recall where he had heard it. To assist him, the black beauty reached to a shelf and pulled a title from it. "You've probably not read it," she told him as she shrugged.

He took the book and looked at its title stamped in black on the yellow board: *The Stairway in the Crypt.* "I've not read it, but I have noticed it here, among Ephraim's books, and have actually pulled it down to scan its pages. He is going to loan it to me eventually. I didn't know you two were acquainted – you've not signed it for him."

"I never sign my name – an elder superstition. That is my one attempt at a work of length, but I admit it's a bit disjointed, more of a collection of inter-connected vignettes and prose-poems than an actual novel; yet the theme is consistent throughout."

"And is the title metamorphic, and is the crypt in fact a symbol of the human psyche, the depths of which we enter at our peril?"

She took the book from him and returned it to its place. "In fact, the stairway leads upward, into a little room – in life, I mean, the place that served as inspiration. You know of the shunned church, on the hill?"

"You mean the one that lost its steeple in that violent storm of last summer? Yes, I can see it, actually, from my study window, although I live a little distance from it on another hill. Ephraim has told me of its haunted legend – well, hinted of that legend merely; I don't think he knows much about it in fact. But now I understand his comment that had me rather mystified, that he wanted to set a story there but that someone had beat him to it."

"He knows that he can still write his little tale, for I invented an alternative setting that no one would mistake for its inspiration. We were going to investigate it together, Ephraim and I; but once we actually stood near it, he became mentally disturbed, spoke of the way the dark vapors of the neighborhood were unnatural and sentient, and that the unwholesome odor of the place reminded him of a smell he experienced in a dream about his own tomb, and other nonsense. So we did not enter in, although I found that a back door was unlocked."

"And you did not return on your own?"

"Never in the waking realm – but I've been there, in my haunted dreams. Well, you came into this room to be alone, I think. You are not a social beast as is our foolish friend. Good evening, Mr. Koffen." He prepared to bow to her, but stopped as he experienced a bizarre and brief hallucination. As he gazed at her, the woman's face tilted just a little, as if it were a mask that had lost its hold. At the same time the entire room blurred around him, as if it belonged to a different dimension – only the magnificent black woman before him kept a solid form. He shut his eyes momentarily, and when again he opened them Miss Rableau was gone – except for the phantom of her face, an image that seemed stained upon the window in the wall. But as he studied the image, it melted into night.

XV.

I cornered Ephraim and told him that I was leaving early due to a headache. He smiled at the lie, knowing my anti-social ways, and thanked me for deigning to show up at all. Holding up *The Stairway in the Crypt*, I asked if I could take it with me and keep it for a wee while.

"Oh sure. She's here, you know – somewhere…" He glanced around the room with intoxicated eyes. Kissing his cheek, I bade him adieu and went to wait for my cab; but as I took my seat and buckled up, I had a sudden impulse, and I gave the driver an address that was not my own. I had the cabbie drop me off some ten blocks from the church.

"You gonna walk around this neighborhood dressed like that?"

"I am indeed," I responded, giving him a handsome tip. "Happy Halloween." He shrugged and shook his head, and then drove off. I coughed at the expulsion of exhaust that billowed from his departing vehicle. The moon, half full, was accompanied by many points of starlight, and the sight so enchanted me that I began to whistle as I walked. I held Miss Rableau's book to the half-moon's glow and spoke its title to the stars. There was no cosmic response. No one was around, which I thought odd, it being a big party night. But as I looked around and observed the state of the houses that I passed, I decided this was an extremely poor neighborhood, and perhaps a dangerous one as well, and that street life was kept to a minimum. It was a cool autumn evening, but I was so overdressed in my Poesque costume that I was quite comfortable, and I grinned at the idea of someone encountering me on the darkened street and their possible reaction to my guise. I reached out at the high fence of black iron that I passed, through which I could see a little courtyard and its fountain, and then I stopped. Before me, a figure reclined on a rough-hewn stone bench. He was dressed in rags and shivered slightly as he slept, and I couldn't comprehend why his face looked so odd until I stepped nearer and saw the pennies that had been placed over his eyelids. I silenced my tune and shut my mouth, but after a little while the gentleman's lips compressed, and he himself began to whistle. Something about the sound filled me with slight panic, for in my wild imagination it seemed that the fellow wasn't whistling – I imagined that his sound was meant to serve as signal to some unseen thing. And my blood iced when, from some distant place, there came a low response of something howling to the moon.

"You come to take me home?"

He had lifted himself onto one elbow and now held his pennies in one palm. "I beg your pardon?"

"I never seen you as dressed in red, thought you'd be all black. Where's your coach?"

I understood. "No, dear fellow, I am not that grim escort. I'm merely in costume, for a party I attended. I am Plague, Death's predecessor." I heard the trickling splash of fountain water and began to move away so as to enter the quadrangle.

"Take this," he called, handing me one of his pennies. "Make a wish."

Accepting his alms, I muttered my thanks and stepped into the courtyard, wherein the moon seemed subtly brighter, so that my flowing shadow preceded my stride. Floating to the fountain, I lowered onto its circular edge and peered into its pond. How strange that the mutated shadows of clouds floated beneath the water's surface, and how queer that one of those shadows looked familiar as it paused in its route to watch me. It was blacker than night, that sphere, and from one end a filigree of stringy crimson vines wavered in the water. Setting down my book, I removed my scarlet gloves and reached into the water. The thing I extracted from the depths was chilly to the touch, and disturbingly soft; and I did not fancy the way its flow of tendrils wrapped around one finger. I held her black visage to moonlight as it dried in risen wind, and I almost brought the faux mouth to my own. She was beautiful, and beguiling; and I could not resist bringing the mask of Marceline Rableau to my face and pressing its underside to my flesh, to which it sensuously cohered. The moon darkened in the gulf of night as from some distant place a thing bayed to blackness.

XVI.

He approached the Cyclopean building and drank its quality of bizarrerie, entranced by the wisps of thick mist with which the building was sheathed. Lifting his eyes, he peered through the eye-openings of his mask and studied the black tower at the building's height, which had not been repaired from the storm damage that had resulted in the destruction of the church steeple. A back door, unlocked, led him into a spacious cellar that was crowded with many disfigured and discarded statues of what he supposed were saints. They were a motley assembly now, with hands pressed together in prayer beneath faces that had in many cases been shattered by some degree of violence. He climbed the worn wooden steps that took him upward, pushing aside the cobwebs with which the cellar was festooned. Reaching the ground floor, Koffen ignored the impulse to check out the nave and sanctuary and found the spiral staircase that took him up to what he imagined to be the bell tower. He absentmindedly noticed that this section of the building was free of grime and spider mesh, and he wondered why the temperature so increased as he climbed. Now and then he passed by murky windows, through which he glanced so as to view the hill on which he had an apartment from which, in twilight's violet half-light, he could see the church and its ruined tower. He could see nothing now except a vague hint of blurring points of electric light in the distance.

He reached at last the tower room, a space of fifteen square feet of five walls, and on each wall there was an austere lancet window, the glass of which was so sooty that he could not see through them. On a table near the entranceway he found an antique oil lamp that lacked its glass chimney, and it thrilled him, as he struck a match and touched its flame to the wick, to see that the old thing still functioned and contained fuel. In the middle of the room stood an irregularly angled stone pillar four feet in height, on which had been chiseled curious alien hieroglyphs. On this pillar rested an obsidian statuette of a figure that seemed attired in Egyptian fashion and donned a nemes headcloth such as was worn by Pharaohs. Peculiarly, the figurine had no face. He ran a finger against the smooth surface that lacked visage, and realized that he had left his scarlet gloves at the courtyard's fountain.

Koffen went to the place where a small bookcase leaned, set down his lantern and Miss Rableau's book. He frowned at the titles of the tomes he found there on the leaning bookcase, weighty volumes that coated his naked hands with debris when he picked them up. Most of the titles, such as the *Liber Ivonis* and *De Vermis Mysteriis* defied his comprehension – but one, the *Cultes des Goules*, had sinister connotations. None of these or the other books on the shelves were in languages that he knew, and so, having retrieved his oil lamp and the woman's book, he turned away from the nameless library and glanced at the high conical ceiling. He wondered why someone had fastened, to two crossbeams above the stone pillar, a series of seven spheres that hung over the figurine; and he did not like the way his eyes lost their focus as he peered at those iridescent globes that caught the refraction of the light from his lantern. Why was the air of the confined room so humid? He did not like the silence of the place, and so he opened *The Stairway in the Crypt* and found a page from which to read aloud. He could feel his warm breath hit the hide of his mask and return into his mouth; but his words arose, to the seven spheres of queer radiance, which began to hum as almost indiscernible threads of lightning shot between them.

Thunder sounded outside the tower chamber, and with it came the smell of storm. He held his lantern's glow to one of the tall, lean windows and frowned at the opaque soot with which that window was covered – for the view afforded if he could have looked through it would have been interesting. He touched a hand to the thick glass and shivered, for unlike the hot room the glass was frigid, unnaturally so. Inclining to the window, he blew his breath upon it and grimaced as the place his hot inhalation touched grew darker still. And then he saw the hazy semblance on that pane of murky glass – the smudge that took on form and became what he first mistook for the reflection of his feminine mask. But when the icon smiled, he sensed that it was other than his false veneer, and when it spoke his name he was certain. That sound was accompanied with another peal of thunder, and he bent momentarily so as to set lantern and book upon the clean floor of the haunted room.

He rose and saw that the image on the window's dusky glass watched him still. How enticing, her mesmeric mouth. How evocatively she murmured his name, like some bewitching lover. How inviting, the mirrored maw. How could he refrain from touching his lips to hers? Yet the moment he did so, he realized his error, as his mouth cemented to the ebon window, through which his essence was sucked into the void.

XVII.

I climbed the stony snow-enshrouded steps that led up the incline of Kingsport's hillside burying ground. Frigid air stung my ears, but I did not mind; for in this quiet place I found solace and escape. I was alone in the place as I climbed to the apex and looked down upon the sleepy seaport town, over the roofs that huddled all around, and the small-paned windows that lit up, one by one, as twilight deepened into dusk. There was no moon, but the gulf of night was a blanket of sparkling stars. It was as I watched those stars that I noticed the dark ethereal form that crept across the sky. I caught my breath and felt afraid, for I had seen this shape in troubled dreaming – a daemon that spun like a hungry thing as it coiled nearer to my eyes and stole their light. I shut my eyes and tried to ease my breathing, and when I scanned the skies again I saw that the daemon had altered in shape and was beginning to break apart. It was a cloud above me, nothing more. And I knew in that instant that there were no deities of rarest air, that such things existed merely in the songs of poets, in the ranting of lunatics and fools. There was nothing but this plot of death, and its quietude, and the unyielding ground on which I stood, as implacable as mundane reality.

The Boy with the Bloodstained Mouth

I saw him in the smoky room, leaning against the pockmarked wall, indifferent to the noise and fumes. His thick dark glasses hid his eyes. I do not think he wore them for any reason of fashion; rather, I think they were meant to conceal his eyes. Oh, how I longed to gaze into those secret eyes. Ah, what revelations might there be revealed, in the eyes of a beautiful boy? He turned his face to mine, and I felt certain that he had noticed my fascinated attention. He smiled as he studied me. Flames of mad desire consumed my weary soul.

I went to him.

His hair was chaos, a mess of black and crimson rat tails that protruded from pale scalp.

His mouth was stained with wet red blood.

Oh, that crimson liquid! How it gleamed in the misty blue light of the place. It clutched my soul.

My fingers caressed his brow, the flesh of which was like ice. He took my hand in his. Leaning to him, I kissed his lips.

I kissed the boy with the bloodstained mouth. I felt nothing as our lips met, no rush of desire, no flame of ecstasy. And when I backed away, I gasped in confusion. His expression had not altered; but his mouth, clean and unstained, mocked me horribly.

And when I licked my lips, I screamed with awful horror.

The Woven Offspring

My brother Alexander and I were not native-born of Sesqua Valley, but we had dwelt within her haunted shadow since infancy; we knew her well. My brother had always been a wild, unruly beast, much like his father before him. Before father's early death, he and Alex would often visit the poisoned patch of land near Mount Selta, the place that feels too deeply the shadow of the twin-peaked mountain. After father's suicide, my brother would vanish for days at a time, and I knew from the lingering shadows in his eyes that he had been to that site where diseased shadow crept into his pulsing heart and altered his sanity. I loved my brother dearly, but ours was a relationship built on pain.

We watched our native-born friends leave the valley when they came of age, so as to journey to other places and learn the secrets of the world. I had no desire to leave the land, and I felt a sense of panic when, in his twenty-third year, Alexander announced that he would be leaving so as to spend time away from home. He was gone for months, during which time I had no word from him. Although he was now a man, he acted so like a child, obstinate and with his mental cache of secrets. I was not, then, surprised when he suddenly returned to Sesqua Valley; but what startled me was that he was not alone, having brought with him a young man named Thomas. Despite his new friend's youth, Thomas had about him an authentic and profound world-weariness. An aspect of pain haunted the lad's beautiful face, and I knew the origin of the needle marks on his arms. To see those same marks on my brother's arm caused me to tremble with subdued hysteria. I knew that I could say nothing, and when Alex begged for money, I gave it to him. He and Thomas would leave the valley for a day or two, and then return with more of the stuff that dulled their mental misery.

Thomas *had* been a victim of the world's cruelty, but my brother's "suffering" was not authentic. His madness gave him no pain; he was merely playing a part so as to impress his beautiful lover. But Thomas was not fooled; he had lived too long among the genuine victims of heartless society. The young man loved my brother, I suppose, and was certainly amused by him. However, his real passion was for heroin. He would sometimes show me a lump of the dirty substance, trying to tempt me to join their ecstasy of habit. I was never enticed. The sight of that dry and filthy poison turned my stomach. I found Thomas, one evening, sitting alone on one of the stone benches in our back garden. His shockingly beauteous grey eyes were glazed, and I knew that he was, as he phrased it, "smacked out." He was gazing unblinkingly at the silver moon. The long sleeves of his black shirt hid the scars on his arms. I sat next to him.

"I love how the moon looks over this valley, Alma." His low voice spoke in whispered words. "Over the city the moon looks so dead and ugly, kind of mocking. I hate it, hate how it watches me and sneers. But here, damn, it's awesome; so silver and majestic. Look at how those soft beams drift to the mountain, at how the white stone seems to drink them in. So cool." Without thinking I ran my fingers through his thick hair. He took my hand and brought it to his mouth. I trembled at his tender kiss. "Your brother's crazy, Alma."

"I know."

He shrugged. "It's cool. I like crazy. I like Alex, but he's into some weird shit. He's giving me an education. Funny, though, I can't seem to shake off this weird feeling of doom." He tried to laugh, as if making a joke, until he saw my expression. I took his hand and touched it to my mouth, kissing the stains on his fingers.

"Not to worry, Thomas. I'll look after the both of you." Yet even as I spoke the words I shivered with chilly uncertainty. I, too, had a sense of foreboding.

A few weeks later the disaster struck. I heard from my bedroom window someone weeping in the garden. Looking out, I saw Alexander lamenting over the body of his friend. I fled my room and rushed to my brother's aid, but he pushed me away violently. I sank to bended knee and stared at the vomit on which the boy had choked to death, his face now resting in its squalid pool. My bones began to shake as Alexander wailed in woe.

We buried Thomas in the burying ground where outsiders to the valley are interred. Alex seemed lost and more unhinged than ever, and I realized for the first time how much his love for the city lad had meant to him. He began to spend much time in the old brick tower which serves as athenaeum for Simon Gregory William's extraordinary collection of arcane lore. It was a place that Alex had visited with father when our mad sire lived. Against better judgment, I stepped one moonless night through the tower's threshold and climbed the worn stone steps to its spacious circular room. I could hear my brother's uttered chanting. I found him sitting in a circle of candlelight, a book of magick in his lap. I watched as he sliced with ritual knife the flesh of his palm, etching into the ripped flesh an alchemical signal that he copied from a chart in the book before him. Quietly, I hunkered to the floor and shuddered at the expression on his face, at his twitching lips, at the heavy glaze of his eyes.

"What are you doing, brother?"

"Hush! Can you hear it?" He waved his bloody hand toward the woodland that surrounded the timeworn edifice. "The trees breathe uneasily tonight." He held his hand to me and chuckled. "We're in luck. The Old Ones smile on us, granting boon. Say his name with me, girl. Thomas, Thomas, Thomas." I rose on shaky limbs and vacated the place. Leaning against a heavy tree, I wept in darkness as valley wind rose in power. Beneath the noise of storm I thought I detected father's mocking laughter.

Afterward, Alexander began to sit in the garden at evenings, knitting needles in hand, a ball of yellow yarn in his lap. I could hear his whispered mantra carried to me on the wind. Occasionally he would dig with one needle into the symbol carved on his palm, and then hold that palm to heaven and bring a strand of dark hair to it. I watched as he drenched the hair with his gore. I listened as he spoke his lover's name. Finally, one evening, I went out to the garden and observed his ritual. I was surprised by his kind smile. The ball of yarn lay next to him on the bench, and in his hand he held a thick strand of human hair. Seeing me stare at that hair, he giggled. "It's amazing what a little corpse hair can accomplish." Leaning to me, he thrust the hair beneath my nostrils. "It smells of him, doesn't it?"

"Yes."

"Yes." He took it from me and picked up the thing he had been making, his doll of yellow yarn. I saw the strands of bloodstained hair that had been twined into the tiny thing. "I'm weaving a conjuration of memory, sister. I'll share it with you once it's completed. You loved him too, I know."

I stared into his moonlit eyes and did not recognize the one before me. Seeming to sense my distress, his eyes grew wild. Suddenly, he held one of the knitting needles threateningly before my eye. A low growl issued from some deep place in his throat. And then his body convulsed and contorted. Madly, he stabbed the needle into his stained palm. Gasping, crying, he held that hand to starlight and chanted again and again his dead one's name. I saw the moon's refracted light darkened in my brother's eyes, and so I raised my eyes to heaven and watched the purple clouds that formed before that satellite of dust, as Alexander's chanting seemed to echo in the gulf of night. And then I heard my brother's cry, and looked on him with horror as he jabbed the needle's point into his neck, savagely, repeatedly, until he dangled on his knees like some frail puppet. I tried to catch him as he tilted in death, but horror had weakened me and so I let him fall to earth as his blood bedewed my garments.

I could not moan or move, and so I sat in heavy silence until I heard, faintly, one peculiar whisper of sound. I sensed weird movement on the earth, next to one of my brother's hands – the hand that had held his woven representation. It moved there, in the unearthly mixture of light and darkness that fell from the muttering sky; and then one mauve moonbeam fell upon it, and I crept nearer so as to watch and smell it, the little idol of yarn and blood and dead man's hair. I watched it raise one tiny arm toward the sky, weakly, as it trembled like some hatchling fallen from a nest. The words that were repeated, vaguely, in the sky seemed to form like images within my mind, and I could feel them spill from my brain to my mouth. Reaching for the needle, I pulled it from its place deep within my brother's neck. I touched that needle's point to nose and mouth, so as to savor carnage. I plunged that needle, at last, into the thing of yarn that writhed before me on the earth, and I laughed as it shuddered with increase of sentience.

Yes, my brother, I had loved the city lad; and so I removed the needle from the woven thing and lifted the nameless eikon with my smooth and bloodstained hands. I brought it to my mouth and breathed hot living aether onto it. And I will tend to it, my brother, as you might have done in saner moments had you not perished. I will nourish it with blood and magick, and care for it for all my numbered midnights.

The Tangled Muse

I.

Sebastian Melmoth lounged on his divan as Max Romp peered at him and sketched impressions onto a pad. The smoke from Sebastian's opium-tainted cigarette rose in whorls that shaped themselves suggestively before his large face; and as he studied their cryptic designs his mouth curled as if to suggest some secret amusement in his mind, and then his breath of laughter pushed the haze away.

"I confess that I'm a bit anxious about your portrait, Max. Your caricatures are so cruelly honest, so offensively true-to-life. They show a distinct want of imaginative exaggeration. You hold your mirror up too close to Nature."

Ada Artemis stood beside a bronze statue of Bast and admired its inlaid blue-glass eyes. Her eyes were of a clear and almost-colorless grey; Sebastian had often complained that such eyes contained no secrets, that nothing could be hidden within such pellucid organs. A woman of few words, she silently watched the scene before her as her hand stroked the surface of the goddess.

Max set down his pen and pad and went to a table on which there was a decorative decanter of sherry. Carefully, he filled a delicate glass with the wine and sipped, and then he walked to where a full-length portrait of a beautiful young man sat on an upright easel. "The same can't be said for this, Sebastian. No one could really be that beautiful. Where did you find it?"

"It's been in my family for generations, on the Wotten side. I never told you that I am descended from aristocracy on my father's side. The painting is a family curiosity, a damaged thing kept in attics for decades, discarded and forgotten. My great Uncle Sebastian, after whom I am named, was especially obsessed with it, so family legend relates, and used to sit in a small dark room talking to the thing. I have told you of him, Ada, the uncle who went mad and spent his final years in an asylum. On the evening of his last madness, for which he was confined, he was found shrieking at the painting and slashing at the figure's breast with a silver dagger. Seems the thing was giving him bad dreams. No one bothered with repairing the canvas – indeed, the family took an active dislike to the thing and kept it hid, perhaps linking it to the mental destruction of a once-beloved relation." Sebastian shrugged. "It eventually came to me, and I had it repaired. The original frame has been lost, no doubt having been used for some other work while this delightful boy was doomed to collect dust in tiny hidden rooms. I brought him with me when I first came to Gershom. I have yet to find a frame suitable for so perfect a representation of youthful beauty. His expression – it breaks my heart. Such a wistful look, almost touching on some vague sadness. What do you think, Sphinx?"

Ada walked to the painting and stood directly in front of it. As a painting it was superb, but she did not care for its subject. There was, beneath the boy's sad eyes, a taint of peevishness; she did not care for the way the fingers of one hand curled, imagining that she saw in them something cruel and clutching. Ada turned to the divan, but before she could disappoint her host with her reply, a young man rushed into the room, hastily removing hat and coat and handing them to the servant who followed him, but keeping a small leather portfolio that he gripped in one long hand.

"Sorry I'm late, Sebastian. I had a sudden brainstorm and got lost working on a new illustration, and that always makes me lose track of time." He then noticed the others in the room who were observing him and became silent, a bit of color coming to his complexion.

Sebastian rose from his divan and went to embrace the boy. Turning to the others he said, "I introduce Japheth Beardsley, a new resident to our city, whom I observed sketching at his table in the Café Regal, much to the chagrin of his maître d'. The sketch was quite grotesque, and very fine. I immediately introduced myself, and we became instant friends."

The others looked at the young man, taking in his threadbare clothes, his gauntness, the hatchet face below the oddly cut chestnut hair. Finally, Ada moved from the painting, approached Japheth and took his hand. "We're pleased that you could join our little *soirée*. I am Ada Artemis. Sebastian says you sketch?"

"He has a remarkable talent for diabolic scenes," Sebastian crowed, "which got him into a bit of trouble in his hometown. Thus he has found his way to Gershom, where he will find neither judgment nor condemnation."

"You exaggerate, Sebastian, as always," said Max, who strolled to the boy and introduced himself. "You've only just criticized my art!"

"What I mean is, we do not critique personality. We do not hound or harass because one's art is morbid. We do not moralize; we know that art can express anything."

"And have you been hounded?" Ada asked the young artist.

Japheth laughed lightly and ran his exceedingly long fingers through his hair. "My first exhibition caused a bit of a scandal," he replied, smiling sheepishly. "I did some panels based on Baudelaire, which some found too – risqué. I found it all rather hypocritical; and so I've come to your city, the legend of which is whispered among various artistic circles with whom I am acquainted."

"I have seen his various *fleurs du mal* and they are quite poisonous," Sebastian said as he lit another cigarette. "Will you have some sherry, dear boy?" He waved toward the table and its decanter.

"Yes, thank you." He glanced about the room and then started as he saw the full-length portrait that had been their topic of discourse. He stepped to it and stared, and then he reached to touch one of the painted hands. Sebastian approached him and lightly touched his shoulder, and then handed him a glass half-full of drink.

"What a wonderful expression haunts your eyes, dear boy. You are enraptured."

"It's just so strange – to see her painted as a young man."

"Her?"

"Audre Brugge, the Belgian girl who sings French songs at *Café Bacchus*. Perhaps you don't know it; it's a bit of a dive."

Sebastian exhaled a plume of perfumed smoke. "Ah yes, the

speakeasy on Queer Street. I was there *once* – the food was awful. I think I know of whom you speak, a pale mulatto wench with polypoid hair. I merely glanced at her, and did not like her voice when she began to warble. I have never heard such a *sepulchral* sound: it was like the voice of one who has tasted death and understood the meaning of that taste. I do not like to think on matters *in extremis*. How you can compare her with this Adonis I cannot comprehend. She was swarthy and alien – and he! He is composed of milk and rose leaf. He is Hyacinthus, beloved of Apollo, and I worship him."

"How are they alike?" asked Ada.

"Their faces are identical, uncannily so. Wait." Japheth drained his glass and set it on a nearby stand, and then he opened his portfolio and rummaged through various papers until he found the desired item. He handed the sheet to Ada, who examined the portrait that had been sketched onto it.

Max joined her and studied both sketch and painting. "Yes," he said, nodding, "she could be Viola to this portrait's Sebastian. Youth is often delightfully androgynous. But what odd hair she has, like coils flowing from the domes of Ceto's daughters. I'm quite intrigued. Does she perform tonight? Shall we go and listen?"

"Don't be absurd, Max," Sebastian huffed. "You haven't finished working on your sketch." He turned to Japheth. "Max is doing my portrait in lithograph."

"I have enough of it to work on – and I have my living model. Come on, this is too fantastic, to find a twin to your ancestor's mysterious portrait. How can you resist?"

"'No, no, go not to Lethe, neither twist
Wolf's-bane, tight-rooted, for its poisonous wine.'"

Ada turned to face their host. "I, for one, am intrigued. Let us go. Japheth will act as our Charon, our son of Night."

Max clapped his hands excitedly. "We shall share a bottle of *Artemisia absinthium* and drink in honor of your sister, Luna," he told Ada excitedly. "Come on, Melmoth, don't be a bore; do join us."

Sebastian yawned dramatically. "Oh, very well. Let me find a book that will be suitable for reading aloud during bad music." He stalked to a section of poetry, scanned the titles and pulled out a volume of *Chants de Maldoror*. "Yes, this will do for so delirious an expedition."

96

Stepping to his closet, he pulled out the long and antique fur coat that was his favorite possession and flung it over his shoulders, and then he held out his hands in a gesture of ushering his company from his rooms.

They stepped into the moonlit night and Ada linked her arm with Japheth's. The young artist's sharp features caught in a peculiar fashion the beams of lunar light, and his pale face seemed almost to glow as he led the way. A heavy gust of winter wind suddenly pushed toward them as it sailed between the city's tall buildings.

Sebastian hugged his heavy coat closer to his frame. "Can you sample it on the wind," he queried, "the taste of doom? Shall we moan to the half-moon like some pack of underhounds?"

"Let us relish what promises to be a new experience," Ada answered.

"Ah, Sphinx – ever the optimist."

They came to Queer Street, and Japheth led the way into a dilapidated house situated between two taller edifices. Gales of laughter spilled from the doorless entrance as they climbed the steps that led onto a long porch, on which various persons sat at tables, drinking and smoking. Sebastian took a cigarette from its gilded case and lit up, which made him feel a little more relaxed. The crowd was mostly young, which pleased him, although he knew that these children had not kept their lives free and inviolate; otherwise they would not dwell within this realm of exile and dispossession, this city of wild unrest. For a moment he remembered his past life, his glory and fame and freedom, his social conquests and his sexual subjugations wherein he was dominate in all things. When his secret life had become known by the society he had courted, they hurled him from their midst. The memory of his rise and fall was his deep-felt damnation; no matter how he reconstructed his former life in this ghastly city, he would never again know the delicious taste of former victory. He walked this realm of living death, a shadow of what once he was.

"Let us find a booth," Sebastian commanded. "I am famished for alcohol."

They settled into leather benches at a table of substantial size. "A bottle of absinthe," Max told their waiter.

"Two bottles," Sebastian corrected him. "And I shall have some coffee laced with a liberal dose of brandy. Anyone else?"

"I'll try some, I guess," Japheth said as he scanned the drink menu and studied prices.

"My treat, dear boy," Sebastian cooed, rewarded with the young artist's thankful smile.

Thus they drank their sweet coffees and bitter booze and talked of art as the young illustrator allowed them to examine his portfolio. When the surrounding chatter quieted, Japheth looked up and saw the woman who watched him as she sauntered past their table and walked to where a blind boy sat before a piano. The room listened as the lad began to play his somber music, and something clutched at Japheth's heart as Audre Brugge began to sing Baudelaire's "La Muse malade." Sebastian forgot his drink and felt his slow-beating heart grow weighty with woe. He began to chant the words with whispered voice.

"Ma pauvre muse, hélas! qu'as-tu donc ce matin?"

"Hush, Melmoth," Max scolded.

"Her voice is like the coming of Death. No, I cannot listen." Sebastian rose and vacated the room, stepping onto the porch and puffing furiously at his cigarette. His companions sat, transfixed, their eyes and ears bewitched. The woman's voice was deeper than Japheth had remembered. Her eyes, those colorless orbs, penetrated him with their staring, and her perfect mouth made love to the language she uttered. The artist, his hands itching for his pen, took in her mauve skin, her coils of tawny hair; and he marveled at how luxurious that hair looked in the misty light of the place, how it seemed in his imagination at times to writhe with an almost lecherous sentience. He watched as her hands trembled to the emotion of her song as they stroked her velvet vest, and he stared at the dark nipple of an exposed breast. Her song ended, and the room exploded with wild applause. Japheth blushed as the lithe chanteuse winked at him and licked her lips as she exited the room.

Sebastian Melmoth felt the presence behind him, one that commanded him to turn and acknowledge. He refused to do so and stared at the yellow moon as if that sphere of dust would grant him inner strength.

"Have you another cigarette?" a husky voice asked. He watched as Audre Brugge moved to a lower step and stood before him. How eerie that the poisonous light of the dead moon seemed to have been transferred to the eyes that held him. Hypnotized, he reached into his vest pocket and brought forth his golden cigarette case. He watched as the woman made her selection and placed the reed of nicotine into her mouth; and he trembled as she bent to him and touched the tip to his. "Your breath tastes of wormwood," she stated, "lots and lots." He detected a Dutch inflection in her accented voice.

"Yes," he replied. "One must imbibe to fulfillment. The first glass will show you things as you wish they existed; and the second glass gives you a glimpse of things as they are not. The third glass of absinthe -- reveals the truth behind the mask of reality, and that is the most horrible of revelations."

"And what do you see behind my mask?"

He sucked deeply on his bit of nicotia and exhaled a patch of scented fume that floated as curtain between them. "Nay, Medusa, your alchemy cannot touch me. My heart turned to stone ages ago."

Secretly she smiled, licked her mouth and walked away.

II.

Sebastian sat on a large gold armchair and looked around the dreary room. Why were the dens of artists always so *cluttered*? Such disarray disconcerted him – he wanted to call for servants. In fact, he was trying to avoid glancing at the large canvas on which Japheth was working at his new project, a life-size portrait of the gorgon that had so beguiled him. But Sebastian could not keep his eyes away, for the artistic process fascinated him. Striking a gold-tipped match, he lit a cigarette and waved it toward the canvas.

"The skeletonic tree is quite good, especially the way it subtly imitates her stance. Of course, you need a moon casting its dead light upon her coils of hair; and the moon must not be white, but rather it must reflect the tainted color of her curious flesh, her reptile hide. Jesu, how like a lamia she looks! She makes one want to quote Keats:

'Where palsy shakes a few, sad, last grey hairs,
    Where youth grows pale, and spectre-thin, and dies;

Where but to think is to be full of sorrow
And leaden-eyed despairs…"'

"Why does she affect you so, Sebastian? I thought you treasured beauty and youth. Look at her eyes – so clear and ethereal. How could such eyes fill you with despondency?"

"They are the eyes of one who preys. I suppose the face is fine, but how can one admire it when it is concealed behind those cords of mane?" He stood and looked out of the window, into night. "This room is really quite depressing. Let us go outside and bathe in starlight. You haven't tried one of my recently discovered cigarettes – they will give you a new sensation. I *adore* new sensations. Come, put down your brush and follow me. Your Medusa will await you." Without waiting, Sebastian went to the door and left the room. Laughing softly, the young artist followed him. The winter night was chilly, but there was no wind. Sebastian was waving a cigarette at heaven, where three bats were silhouetted as they flitted in the lunar light. "This sky is positively Goyaesque," he stated. "Of course, we need owls instead of bats. Are you familiar with his *El conjuro*? It would not surprise me to see a pack of disheveled hags hobbling down that street, selling their craft. But – lo! – see where a witch approaches."

He flicked the butt of his consumed cigarette into a gutter as Audre Brugge approached them; and for one moment she did seem like something conjured by black arts, with the strange moonlight giving her skin a poisonous viridian tinge. Japheth saw how her helical hair seemed to move and arrange itself as she advanced toward them – and that was odd, for there was no wind. She stopped before them.

"Good evening, gentlemen," she said, one hand holding the bottom of her small shoulder bag.

"My dear Miss Brugge. How like a viper you look in that tight dress, with its geometric pattern. Would you care for a new sensation? I've just received these, from a friend in Mozambique." Sebastian reached into a pocket and produced a black cigarette case, which he snapped open. "They will make you dream tonight," he promised her.

"No thank you, Monsieur. I want to taste the evening air, it's so rich tonight."

Sebastian snapped shut the case without offering a weed to

100

Japheth. "As you wish. I shall leave you then, for I too wish to dine on this intoxicating effluvium. I suppose you wish to be alone in his little room and pay homage to the gods of Art."

"Actually – no." The woman smiled at Japheth. "There's a curious place I want to show you, just outside the city perimeter. I think it will interest you, from an artistic standpoint."

"All right," the young man agreed.

"If you're going to walk the night then I shall follow, surreptitiously and from a distance. I shall be your voyeur and watch in secret."

The woman laughed and linked her arm with Japheth's, and Sebastian slowly followed as they walked beyond the city, to a place of ancient desolation. Perhaps, aeons ago, it had been some kind of park, although its trees were few and withered, like something found in Casper David Friedrich; and Japheth felt a kind of pity for the barren trees, for their limbs seemed bent with heavy desolation. Sebastian scowled at the dreary wasteland as he followed the younger mortals up a slight incline to where the remnant of a ruins stood. Audre stopped before a weathered arch that was guarded by a statue of Cerberus, and she smoothed her hand over one of the daemon's three monstrous heads.

"Wait," Sebastian wailed as the woman walked past the beast and began to descend a set of steps that led to a circular platform of stone. "I have no honey cakes with which to placate the hound. If we step into its lair we may ne'er return!"

"Be not afraid, Monsieur. I shall be your Aeneas and pacify the fiend." She held her hand to Japheth. "Come," she commanded.

But Sebastian was suddenly overwhelmed with fear. He had not, in all of his years in Gershom, dared to leave the city's boundaries; being out of it now instilled a kind of panic, a sense of terror. Holding his hand up in protest to the woman's invitation, he turned and fled.

Japheth tried to laugh. "He has the oddest habit of *fleeing*," he joked; and yet he, too, felt a kind of uncanny fear in the forlorn place. Was it his imagination, or had the atmosphere grown more chilly after they had passed beneath the archway and descended the stone steps? He watched as Audre reclined on the circle of stone and began to trace the shape that was outlined on it with her slim hand. When she reached that hand to Japheth, he took it and lay beside her.

"What is this place?" he asked.

"I don't know. It must have been part of some antique civilization that existed prior to the city, although heaven knows that Gershom is in itself infinitely old. Perhaps this was their temple – it seems a place of veneration, doesn't it? And perhaps this figure chiseled into this circle of stone was the thing they worshiped. You can sense how utterly primitive it is, a relic of a forgotten era; and yet how exquisitely it is captured in their art, whoever it was that dwelt here. I knew it would fascinate you, as an artist. Primeval art has always beguiled me. I like to think about the world as it once was, millennia ago. What did they feel, that we can never sense? What did they know, and worship? What were their *secrets*? We know of the past from what they left recorded – but what were the mysteries unrevealed? It's funny, but when I lay in this place, beneath the antediluvian starlight, I feel near to a nameless past."

"This is an odd figure," he conceded, fingering the thing that was engraven on stone. "It looks like a king, or ruler, by the way it's outfitted in that robe, and by the staff or whatever it is it holds. Can't really tell its gender, but the haughty stance seems belligerently male. It's really weathered here, at where it wears a half-crown or whatever it is. It's superb, certainly. It has an aura of – power." He gazed into her clear eyes, the eyes that held him in their bewitching splendor. "Do you c—come here often?" he stuttered.

"Mmm, yes. It's a great place to lay still, to dream. Will you dream with me, Japheth?" She leaned toward him and briefly touched her mouth to his. "Be still. Here, let me rub some of this onto your temples." She retrieved a tiny jar from her bag and turned open its lid. "It's something I discovered in Tibet." He watched as she dipped two fingers into the jar's gelatinous stuff and sighed as she anointed him. Her mouth was at his ear, sighing strange language that he could not comprehend. He wanted to kiss her eyes but found that he could not move his heavy limbs. No matter. It was wonderful enough to be still and let her love him. She was on top of him, unbuttoning his shirt, and then her nails were etching signals into his chest. When she finally pressed her lips onto his eyelids, he was able to move a little. His opened his eyes, and his hands were on her heavy breasts. She pulled him on top of her and began to hum a strange melody as she allowed him to kiss her mouth, her neck, her nipples.

And then he knew that he was dreaming, as something wet and thin below her breast wrapped around his finger. "It is a gift from him – the Master," she sang in her queer low voice. "It is his reward to his anointed." He moved his head beneath her breast, to where the worm grew from out her flesh, at the place where her diabolic heart pumped. He touched the worm with his mouth, his mouth that opened as the thing stretched its elastic body and slipped between his lips. He sucked as the creature tickled the back of his throat, and when at last it removed itself from his orifice, he tasted the musky slime that coated his stinging lips.

Japheth awakened to the soft moaning of morning wind; he saw the mist above the ruins wherein he lay, in that cold and lonesome place. The siren had deserted him, he was alone; but she had left him with a souvenir. He brought the strand of coiled hair to his nostrils and drank its weird perfume.

III.

Max Romp opened his portmanteau, took out his new sketch and placed it on the table before which he and Ada Artemis sat. "It's *too* grotesque, not at all my kind of thing. It's like something out of Poe, and the style is so bizarre. Usually my sense of line is strong, but this watercolor is all blur and blotch – there are no solid lines. Now the hazy cityscape in the background suggests Gershom, but it's from an angle that I've never personally experienced."

"And you say that you saw this thing in dream?"

"That's right, the most vivid nightmare I've ever experienced. Usually even my wildest dreams have some root in reality – but this thing! It's dark phantasy of the queerest kind. And that sinister tramp or whatever the hell he is, great gods! He stands like some symbol of all the world's outcasts, with his tattered robe and glistening crown.

Ada leaned a little nearer to the work. "Glistening?"

"It shimmered, but with a dull liquid kind of scintillation, like some distant muted starlight. And it seemed to move, as if a sentient thing.

Ugh, I need another brandy!" He stalked to the bar and refilled his empty glass. "And the queerest thing of all was the sound, like some low moaning; a subterranean wind, perhaps, emanating from beneath the ground. Actually, when I reflect on the noise, it sounded a lot like that woman's singing. You know, young Beardsley's mophead muse."

Ada sat back and sipped tea from a delicate china cup, and then she looked up and smiled as Sebastian was let into the room by a manservant. "Coffee! Have you any sobering coffee? Ah, I see it there! Yes, let me help myself to a cup." Ada rose and went to her friend, startled at his disheveled appearance. Her hand gently touched the tall man's shoulder, and he turned to take hold of it. "Sphinx, your hand is hot. Let me cool it with my kisses." He kissed it once and then returned to pouring coffee into a tall cup. Ada reached for the container of cream. "No, no, dear woman. Let us not dilute its potency with cream, nor sweeten it with sugar. No, let me drink it black and strong, and thus dispel the Morphean lure."

Max rose to join them, laughing. "Good god, Melmoth, you're a mess! You look like you haven't slept for days."

Sebastian gulped a scalding cup of coffee as though it were water and then refilled his cup with the dark brew. "Sleep! I have been too perturbed too sleep! I have suffered the *Napoléon* of Nightmares! Why is it so somber in here? We need music. Why have you no musicians at hand, Sphinx, to soothe the soul and ease the mind?" He drained the cup a second time and refilled it once more.

"Hell, Melmoth, settle down. I've had a bad nightmare myself, but I'm not running around all gaga. Sit down and behave yourself."

"Spare me your fatuous criticism, Max. Your nightmare cannot compare to the incubus that sucks my sanity – the little I have remaining. You have not been walking the streets since midnight, haunting cafés so as not to be alone. You have not been to St. Expiry to light a candle for your own soul. I will not sit down and be calm – I will howl with the legion of the damned!" He gulped more coffee.

"Drink slowly, dear, you'll choke," cooed Ada. "Do not be quick to judge our friend. His dream has been unusual and drear."

Sebastian produced a mauve handkerchief and wiped his brow. "Was it, Maximilian? Did you see our city from that horrid desolate place just outside its boundaries, looking like a metropolis of the damned? Did you see the dead trees that *writhed* like semi-sentient things as they hurled their shadows onto your face, your eyes? Did you behold the Lord of Worms rise from his realm of tarnation, clutching his staff of burnt bone and incinerated flesh, with which he etched your name into the dust? Great Jesu, did you see all that?"

Huffing, he strode to a chair and sat, wiping at his pale face, glancing for a moment at the upside-down image of Max's illustration. Then he froze, and his white face drained to a deeper pallor. Silently, his eyes filled with fear, he bent to the drawing and turned it around.

"You neglected to mention the sepia moon, looking like a scab in heaven," Max quietly told him. "I think I'll have some coffee after all. Shall I pour you a brandy, Melmoth?"

"This is uncanny. You've been to this place after all."

"What place?" Ada asked, kneeling next to Sebastian's chair and taking hold of his hand.

"But how can you have witnessed my dream? We have been bewitched. Beardsley's harpy has worked some necromantic foolery over us." He turned to Ada. "The place is just beyond the city. You know I have never left the city in the three decades that I have dwelt here – except for the few times that I have visited the Isle of Moira, wherein the dead are interred. I was bold enough to follow Beardsley and his witch to this place, but I panicked and fled. Your blurry rendition of its ruins is quite haunting, Max. I've never known you to depict places – you must have felt its spectral power when you were there."

"I haven't a clue what you're muttering about, old boy. I haven't set foot out of this city since stepping off the train seven years ago. I would never hike outside its boundaries. I am metropolitan to the bone."

"And you, Sphinx – have you dreamt of this place?"

"You forget, dear friend – I never dream."

"I know that you have told me so, but I never believed it. I prefer my sad dreams to no dreams at all. But this vision that Max and I have shared -- *that* I wish I had never beheld. It is portentous, and nothing good can come of it. I must warn Beardsley."

"Stay and warn him in the morning. Look, the winter darkness comes so early, and I can tell you haven't eaten. Dine with us and sleep here until morning, and then together we can see your friend."

Sebastian rose to his unsteady feet. "How wise you are, dear Sphinx, and kind; but I cannot rest until I have warned my young friend. We have been given a premonition of some evil thing, but it merely brushes us with its wings. The beak is pointed toward a young man's heart. He sits in lamplight, and the daemon that is dreaming spills its shadow over him; and if I do not save him now, his soul from out that shadow will be lifted – nevermore."

IV.

Japheth awoke to the ringing of the bell. Drowsily, he walked down the steps and opened the building's door. Sebastian clasped his shoulders with shaking hands. "Thank the gods that you are here! I've been ringing for five minutes."

"Settle down, Sebastian. Good lord, you look awful. Come in out of the cold. I've been sleeping; soundly, I guess, if I didn't hear your ringing for so long a time." He shut the door and led the way to his dark room.

"Sleeping – perchance to dream?"

"Huh? I don't recall. I think I'm still waking up. Sorry it's so chilly in here, my fire's gone out. Let me tend it. Have you eaten? I'm going to heat up some wonderful soup. You look in need of nourishment."

"Bother nourishment. I've come to warn you of the thing that is feasting on your soul – that harpy!" He pointed to where the painting leaned upon its easel and saw that the canvas was covered with a piece of black velvet. "That's a good sign, Japheth, to hide her from view. But it will be better still to destroy her image. There, your palette knife – it will serve our purpose."

"What on earth are you babbling about, Sebastian? No, put down the knife and answer me!"

The young man was not quick enough to stop the elder fellow from reaching for the black cloth and ripping it away. The knife fell from Sebastian's hand as he saw the thing that mocked him with its baleful eyes. Was it the same painting? He thought that it was, although it had been horribly altered. The creature's flesh shimmered with a kind of liquid coating that glistened in the glow of yellow moonlight. The coils of hair had been altered and did not cover any of the woman's face, the face that was no longer beautiful. Sebastian did not know what he feared the most – the twisting lips or the cruel eyes. He marveled at how the artist had caught an aspect of serpentine movement in the ropy tangles of coiled hair. Behind the creature, in the distance and almost completely hidden in darkness, was another figure, barely discernable. Sebastian knew that the thing wore a tattered robe and crown of worms.

"I've added your moon, per your suggestion. It brings the thing to life, doesn't it? God, I've been working on it all night, right after I awakened from the dream. Little wonder I've slept like the dead. I knew when I awakened that alterations were required. Dreams can be so instructive, don't you find? I've never been able to capture grotesquerie so infallibly. I am nothing if I am not grotesque. What a muse she has been for me!"

It came to them, from outside the window: the harsh low singing. The lad smiled and kissed Sebastian on the mouth, and then vacated the room. Sebastian fell to his knees and would have moaned if he were not too frightened to utter sound. Timidly, he crept to the window on hands and knees, trying to fight the fear that labored to prevent his peering into night. By the time he found the courage to push aside the curtains, the two retreating figures were far away. The poor old fellow clasped his hands together and prayed to the moon.

They walked through winter's chilly air to the ruins outside the city. Hand in hand, they climbed up the slight gradient that led to the ruins. Japheth smiled at the three-headed beast that stood as sentinel before the archway; but then his face grew somber as he looked beyond that archway to the circle of stone -- to that which stood thereon. His companion wrapped her arms around his waist and kissed his ear.

"We've taken a fancy to you. We love your dreaming. It is said that Gershom is a godless place, and perhaps that's true; but there was once religion here, of an ancient kind. We are its avatars. Come, join us. Go to him, Japheth, and kiss his staff."

She released him. Japheth walked down the steps and knelt before the moonlit deity. He could smell the diseased flesh of which the Old One was composed. When he lifted his face to the thing's dark eyes he beheld the crown that was composed of lengthy nematodes, their hermaphroditic bodies knotted as they moved through the Old One's dome. The demigod touched a rotted hand to Japheth's head and pushed his face toward the carrion staff. The young man pressed his lips to the charnel thing as the hand that touched him worked over his tingling flesh. He felt the woman's hands rip at his clothing and knead his flesh, the flesh that began to alter, to shrivel and grow moist. Naked, he buried his face into the woman's moving hair as his flesh began to secrete its slime, the viscous substance that Audre Brugge lapped voraciously as his human body continued to wither and shrink with transmutation.

Dead moonlight cast its diseased illumination upon the Old One, the thing that placed its new acolyte into a writhing crown.

Let Us Wash This Thing

I brought my treasure, wrapped in plastic, to Wormhead's lair and set it before his folded hands.

"Been excavating again, have you?" he queried, not moving to touch my offering. "I cannot say that it is wise, to frolic in the places outside Gershom. The landscape is so unruly."

"Danger gives me a tingle," I answered.

He sighed and grimaced. "You see everything as sexual, harlot. How blasé. The erogenous zone is often such a bore when it is merely appetite."

"It need be nothing more. It serves its purpose."

"Rather philistine, your approach to life. However you were drawn to Gershom I cannot fathom."

"We can't all be poncy aesthetes. Some of us like to have a bit of backbone. And there are no rules about wandering outside city parameters. I don't believe in restrictions, and that's exactly why I've settled in this depraved city. Are you going to look at the damn thing or not?" I took a cigarette from its packet and lit up. The freak finally unraveled his ugly hands and daintily worked the plastic from the relic, and I smiled at the way he sneered in dismay at the object's coat of filth. Still, there was thralldom in his eyes as he was dominated by intense interest, even though he couldn't bring himself to touch the hand of stone. "Well?"

"'Tis certainly absorbing," he lisped. Snapping fingers, he summoned one of his lingering acolytes. "Bring a basin of warm water and some liquid soap. Let us wash this thing." I watched in agitation, and when the basin and brush were brought, I plopped the relic into the water, added the amber soap and worked at cleaning the artifact.

Wormhead couldn't refrain from panting as I toiled, and I used this moment to get as near to him as he ever allowed me to, so that I could smell and study him. His stench was similar to butyric acid, an acrid smell that yet contained an ingredient of syrupiness, sweet and cloying. His dark features and swarthy flesh suggested an element of gypsy in his genetics. But what really captivated the attention was the work of art that had been surgically embedded into his dome, a reed-like garland made of brass forged to resemble an assembly of conjoined worms that wove into and out of his flesh. This funny fellow was one of Gershom's elder residents – indeed, no one, not even those older folk who had lived here most their lives, remembered a time when Wormhead wasn't an inhabitant, and many speculated that he was the only known native of this city of exiles. His art, such as it was, was the art of sorcerer. That's what put the idea into my head when I first found the artifact buried in a field outside the city.

One of Wormhead's little aides handed me a towel, with which I dried the artifact, the thing of dark beauty. The obsidian hand had been superbly sculpted and was a work of smooth ebony. Upon one extended finger it wore a ring of white gold, and on its palm was an opal diagram that caught the light with refractions of myriad colors. Having thoroughly dried it, I placed the article on the table before the freak as the basin was removed. Wormhead touched one finger to the hand and shuddered.

"Its two extended fingers form the Elder Sign, such as one finds in diagrams in ancient tomes." His eyes glimmered as he turned the thing over and ran one talon across the palm. "The insignia there is one I do not recognize. How its colors pierce one's eyes! The ring is a thing of perfect exquisiteness. I have a tiara that is composed of comparable metal. How well did you hunt for the rest of the statue? Surely this was broken from some amazing icon."

"Well enough. I also went to the ruins and explored there, but that place gave me the creeps so I didn't look long." Reaching for the hand, I worked its ring, turning it until it loosened. The mutant watched with suspicious eyes as I worked the hoop of metal from its frigid finger and moved it near his exploratory hand. "This will be your payment," I informed him.

He opened his hand with its palm upward, and into that palm I placed the hoop of gold. "And what am I to perform, for so rare a treasure?"

I stood erect and filled my voice with force. "Your art of conjoining."

For the first time since I had entered Wormhead's realm, he smiled. "Wherever did you hear of that?"

I smiled too. "I've heard whispers of your aid to the blind fool; it's quite a local legend."

"It was ages ago. You know of the legend, but you've never heard the entire fable, I assume."

Something chilly entered into his eyes that I did not like, and the radiance outside the window darkened just a little although I knew the skies were free of clouds. "No, I haven't."

He took hold of the ring and slipped it onto one finger. His red eyes seemed to smolder with inner inferno. Below those eyes, his nose was almost nonexistent, and his lips were too small for teeth that stretched too widely, so that his mug resembled a death's-head. "Once upon a time," he alleged, "there was a blind fool who bumped into the stalls of Gershom's ghetto. No one took pity on him because of his stupidity, and so he spent many hours in the small cathedral of St. Toad's praying for a recovery of sight. I attend St. Toad's myself, to pray to Crawling Chaos in the arcane morning hour of three-o'clock, the time when dead gods listen to the supplications of doomed mortality. I found him there, this wretch in rags, and led him to a font where I washed his blistered feet. 'Why do you pray for eyes?' I asked him, and he replied, 'So that I may weep.' The answer was so beautifully idiotic that I deigned to respond with arcane craft. Nearby there was a sculpture of the effeminate Christ, where I found, embedded in each outheld hand, a ruby of blood-red beauty. With these tough talons, I worked the gems from out their pallid hands, and with these sage lips I uttered prayer of a different sort, and thus worked diabolic wonder. The jewels, sunken into his pits that once held eyes, transfigured into living orbs that kept their gem-like splendor; and through those scarlet spheres he looked upon the world again, and went away to his little ghetto residence. And he looked upon the world of men, and its cruelty, and saw that those who hated him still did so, but now their odium was laced with envy, and fear of the mysterious, as well as with lust for the treasure of his ruby eyes. He looked upon this world and did not weep, for such vileness brought water to his mouth alone and he spat his malcontent. And thus he returned to St. Toad's, where he found a ritual dagger with which to pluck out the crimson gems that were his eyes; and then he thrust that dagger into his wretched heart, and his trivial gasp of death rose as prayer to whatever saint might heed it."

I watched him pick up the relic and kiss its palm. "Now, do you still desire my enchantment?"

I did not hesitate. "I do."

"And whom am I to assist?"

"The poet of hounds."

He mulled this over in his mind. "He has not been long in Gershom. Why has he exiled himself from the world of wretched humanity?"

"They scorned him for praying to the Outer Gods. When it was discovered that he had penned potent psalms to they who dance in the spaces between stars, his writing hand was chopped off and burned upon an altar."

Wormhead balanced the relic between two hands. "You would have me, then, conjoin this to his wounded wrist. I see. Where is his abode?"

"He has a little hole in Poet's Place."

He rose. "Let us away." One of his pygmies brought him a resplendent robe, and he knelt so that it could be fitted around his shoulders. He stayed upon his knees as his two adorers squatted before him and placed pipes into misshapen mouths, and I shivered slightly at the eeriness of their windy canticle. Wormhead listened for a little while, and then he raised a foot and smashed it into one piper's head, and as the two homunculi groveled on the ground, the callous freak ascended and pointed to the relic. I went to wrap it once more in plastic. "No, do not efface it with that vile synthetic shroud. There, that bit of black velvet that covers my crystal sphere – enclose it in that."

I obeyed his command and then followed him from his dwelling, into daylight. I must admit that I enjoyed the way people gawked at us as we strode down the walkways of Gershom. Wormhead was a creature of legend that most people had whispered about but few had seen in flesh. There was nothing arrogant in the manner of his stride, and yet he exuded a power of presence that made people move out of his way with awestruck fear shadowing their eyes. Finally, we reached the derelict edifice that was called Poet's Place, and I escorted the mutant inside and to the landing on which our quarry had a room. We entered to find the poet weeping before a towering statue of Anubis.

"Joseph," I called, and he turned to gaze at us with liquid eyes. Wormhead did not hesitate but walked directly to the poet and lifted the amulet that the fellow wore around his neck. It was a strangely crafted trinket – a small amulet fashioned of dark jade that had been carved into the likeness of what might have been a crouching winged hound, or a sphinx with a semi-canine countenance. I did not like the malevolent expression that was evoked by the curve of the creature's cruel mouth, with its overexposure of teeth – and then I noticed the subtle similarity between the amulet's maw and Wormhead's too-wide smirk.

"Why do you need a second hand to be a poet? You have a mouth, and can warble your verses to the wind."

The poet moved that mouth only. "It would be good to write again, to know the ritual of pen and paper, to see the words form before me as solid language. But that is not the reason I want a hand, my lord. I need a second hand so that I may pray in proper fashion, palm against palm." He lifted his two arms, touched wrist to wrist; and I could almost see the hand that had been lost pressed against the one that yet remained.

"Ah," the fiend hissed. "Then I shall assist you. You know the prayer to Shub-Niggurath, with which to conjure forth her pool of vintage spillage?"

"For that we need a hermaphrodite's blood."

"How convenient, then, that we are attended by such a creature," Wormhead sang, pointing to myself. "On your knees before me, poet. Let us work this wonder." The small man bent before us, hand and stump pressed upon the wooden floor. How oddly Wormhead seemed to rise, as if an extension of inches had been added to his height. His lifted talons to the ceiling and spoke an ancient tongue. I watched, as coils of brightness churned within his eyes. I saw those serpents of light spill from his eyes and copulate, thus forming a swirling pool of radiance. The alchemist stopped his vocal noise and turned to peer into my eyes, and then he grinned and brought one hand to my mouth, and I cried in protest as his sharp talon split the tissue of my lips. My hot blood oozed into and over my mouth. How nastily Wormhead chortled. "Spit into the pool, thou freak of nature," he mocked.

Hatefully, I spat into the churning ectoplasm and watched the pale pool turn to deepest crimson. Wormhead motioned to the poet and reached for the handless wrist, which Joseph dipped into the enchanted pool. Then the mutant held his hand before me. I unwrapped the relic and offered it to the devil, then pressed the velvet cloth to my mouth so as to stop my spillage. How gracefully Wormhead dipped the relic into the pool and touched it to the poet's wounded wrist.

"Wash," Wormhead commanded.

I could not help but watch, enchanted, as the obsidian hand softened and stitched itself into the poet's flesh as he washed within the spectral stuff. At last the pool evaporated into the atmosphere of the dusky room. Joseph moved his midnight hand and raised it to meet Wormhead's mouth, with which the mage kissed the ebon palm. The poet shuddered and then reached for Wormhead's hand on which the monster wore the ring of white gold, the ring to which the poet touched his lips. And then Joseph pressed his hands together – one white, one black – and uttered a Tindolic prayer, which was answered by some distant baying sound.

Wormhead leered at me and spoke my name. I dropped the velvet cloth and pressed my bloodstained mouth to the ring upon his hand; and then, bowing my head, I pressed my palms together.

Bloom of Sacrifice

I.

The figure of obsidian stone wept into the pool of squalid water. The beast of Sesqua Valley pointed to the center of the pool. "There. You see the cluster of flowers that float before the statue? No, do not tremble. If anyone should be afraid it is I. We children of the valley are not welcome on this mountainous region. For me to bring you here is an act of defiance for which I may dearly pay. Still, I revel in disobedience, and I'll swallow my fate. Be not afraid. The water knows that you are here on a mission of merciful love for your brother. It will hold you above its surface."

This weird information did little to calm my nerves. This mountain pool, the odd valley, and Simon Gregory Williams especially disturbed me profoundly. I *was* afraid. Looking into the water, I saw vague and murky figures, shadows or specters I could not say. Simon scowled at these phantasms and spat into the water. I watched the water ripple and darken as the ghostly figures drifted downward and disappeared.

"Now. You must swim to where the flowers float just beneath the Faceless God. As you enter the pool you must pulsate with the adoration you feel for Thomas. Focus on your resolution to assist him, no matter the sacrifice."

"And what kind of sacrifice would that be?"

The beast observed me with his slanted silver eyes. Horribly, he smiled. "I cannot say."

I shut my eyes and conjured forth an image of my brother on his deathbed. I saw him surrounded by candlelight and bouquets. I saw the movement of his mouth as he quietly begged that I help him die. I beheld the lesions on his limbs that he tried to hide with heavy robe. Dull anger and exquisite heartache fumbled deep inside my soul. I wept into the turbid pool. When at last I rubbed my weary eyes, I saw again the distant forms within the water's depths, the figures that seemed to beckon. I removed my clothes and slipped into the water. It was as thick and warm as newly-shed blood. Pushing myself deeper into it, I watched the ripples the surged from me and then returned like a hungry thing. I raised my arms and saw the liquid that sheathed them sink into my tingling flesh, not one drop returning to the pool. With no attempt of my own, I floated toward the statue. I saw the weird dark liquid that shimmered blackly on the surface that should have been a face, an oleaginous substance that fell into the pool. I stopped just before a cluster of dry flowers, horrid dead things that I did not want to touch. Dreadfully, the nearest flower lifted itself and crept to my palm. I raised the desiccated thing to my face and gagged at its stench. Repulsed, I crushed the lifeless floret, then gasped as pain shot through my hand, my arm – then found my numbing brain. A drop of mortal blood fell into the water and sank into the waiting mouth of some lingering phantasm. Vision beclouded, and senses transfigured. I felt as weightless as a whispered word.

Mountain floor chilled my nakedness. I was as dry as the thing I grasped in my aching hand. I scanned the cavern, but the beast of Sesqua Valley had vacated the place. Alone, I tipped toward the pool and gazed into the haunted water. I saw my forlorn reflection sink into the squalid depths, until it disappeared.

II.

A faceless god mocked me in some cosmic place. It sang to me with voices that issued from where a mouth should have been. Wings of black leather spread over twin bodies, and I saw the place where those naked forms were joined at the waist. Daemonic aether rushed around me, haunted by the movement of heavy wings, wings that beat in time to the creature's ancient song. My quivering mouth opened and I cursed the spectral air with hateful song. I sang for centuries, accompanied by the creature joined to my hip. His hand clutched my breast, just above my heartbeat. His moist lips pressed against my own. His curling tongue sank into my throat. My aching phallus stretched toward cosmic nothingness like some thorny vine on which a dewy blossom glistened at its tip. I ripped it from me and gave it to my love. He crushed it to his face and sucked with famished mouth its nectar. With single thrust, he slashed its silver thorns across the flesh that made us one. We stained the cosmos with our blood, and in that crimson flow I watched my brother float from me.

Sobbing, I awakened. I heard the sound of eerie music, and saw the form that held a flute to its wide mouth. It pranced toward me, this beast. Taking the instrument from its mouth, it placed a wide hand upon my brow. "You have such potent dreams, Jeremy. I've packed your clothing, and arranged a ride to your home early this morning. You will take good care of this." Simon handed me a small box composed of teak. I opened the lid and saw the dry floret on its bed of velvet. From some distant place, I heard the sound of baying. Pushing out of bed, I staggered to a window and peered at Sesqua Valley. Even in darkness I could make out the titanic silhouette of the white twin-peaked mountain. I placed my hand upon the chilly pane of glass, and my soul froze. There was no image of the hand that touched the glass. Breathing hard, I bent nearer to the window, as the beast played mocking melody on his damnable flute. I studied the window, and saw the room behind me, the flickering candlelight with which it was illumed. There was no image of myself.

I understood my sacrifice.

What stays with me now is the memory of silence that existed on that magic mountain. It is a memory that calls to me in dream, and I know that I will one day return unto that haunted vale. I have other memories as well, memories of pain and sorrow. I recall the scent of many flowers, the fragrance of magnolia incense, the smoke of which caused Thomas to cough. I remember the way he would laugh at me as I scolded him about that incense. We gazed at each other as I sat beside him on his deathbed. Oh, his brilliant eyes! His face and frame had altered, ravaged by his disease; but his eyes were as magnificent as ever, and therein lived the brother that I loved. Yet even they had been tainted. In youth we had played a game wherein we would stare into each other's eyes, so as to catch our identical reflections. The memory of that game chilled me now. I knew what I would not see were I to look into his eyes for all eternity.

Thomas seemed to sense my stress, and thus I turned to look about the room, which had been decorated by his attempts at art. I saw the many images of a faceless god that wore a triple crown. "Admiring my deliverer, brother? Ah, mighty Nyarlathotep. What promises he makes. Into what a depth of darkness he promises to sweep me, on the day of my happy death."

"Don't be morbid."

"Pah. I'm being existential. I swim toward my inescapable doom. Promise me, Jeremy, that you will toss my ashes from the heights of Mount Selta."

"Don't speak of death. You may live for unnumbered years."

Peevishly, he pouted. "You still refuse to understand. I sent you on a mission, and you performed with perfection. You found the thing of which I read in some volume of misbegotten lore, a tome that I found in the tower at Sesqua Valley. In that tower I was taught secrets by a fantastic beast, and learned of that which would help me expire in wondrous fashion. No, there are no numbered years. There is only now, this moment. There is only this teak box, and the thing that nestled within it."

Fear welled up within me, and he placed an emaciated paw upon my arm. "I don't want to do this," I protested. "Or if I must, I want to share your fate."

"That you cannot do. Damn you, you promised me this. Don't desecrate your vow. Open that box, damn you, and take up the dead thing. Yes, just so." He opened his heavy robe, and I tried not to stare at the lesions on his flesh. "Now, place the dead thing on my chest, just above my heart. There, so easy. And now, my love, kiss your brother goodbye."

Uncontrollably, I shook. My eyes were dim with tears as I bent to him and pressed my mouth to his. Gently, I placed a hand upon his chest, next to the thing from Sesqua Valley. When I took my mouth away, his raspy breathing softened and grew still. Floral perfume wafted about us. I felt a sore beneath my hand smooth with healing. With blurry vision I watched as the brittle flower began to alter, to

118

bloom. There came from its petals a beautiful bouquet, and I gulped the waves of fragrance. They seeped into my nostrils and sank to my pulsing heart. I knew that organ's thud inside my ears and felt it on my brain.

And his. I felt his heartbeat join mine, a brotherly palpitation. I watched his stilled flesh drink in the flower's substance. I watched that flower melt into his meat, that husk of flesh that softened and became beautiful, unblemished. Bending low, I kissed his hair, as my hand found the place above his breast whereon I had placed the magick bloom. I could not take my hand away, and thus I felt that which tore my universe apart: his final heartbeat.

He Who Made Me Dream

Did death, I wonder, carry with it some psychic odor, as opposed to its common stench? Or was it the specter of long-anticipated tragedy that shocked my senses with fear as I touched the doorknob? Some secret intuitiveness prepared me for the ghastly sight. I pushed open the door, stepped into the gloom, felt as though I had walked into the lingering shot of some somber *film noir*; looked at the bed mat that huddled in its corner, the filthy sheets reflecting the blue glow of a digital clock. I was aware of the shadowy thing that slumped in mid-air, but could not yet confront it.

Stepping to our fetish altar, I knelt before it and fingered the leather gear and razor blades, lit candles and burned musk incense. I watched my shadow that was thrown upon a wall. The curling spirals of smoke reminded me of him: his smell, his pale skin. I remembered when we had first made love, at some hidden swamp, where we had fucked to the music of its inhabitants. I saw once more his saturated beauty, the water dripping from the black hair that clung to his face. I heard his necklace of bones clatter with each copulative thrust. Pushing memory away, I reached for the sheathed knife with which we had sliced ourselves while making love. My fingers found the empty sheath. Lifting my eyes, I acknowledged my lover. The altar knife lay on the floor beside the fallen stool. His corpse hung from a length of rotting rope that had been attached to one of the hooks we had fastened to the ceiling. His tilted sunglasses covered the dead eyes. The leather jacket and jockstrap, his only attire, caught the flicker of candlelight, and on his once-lovely mouth were the remnants of crusty blood.

Shutting eyes, I placed moist palms upon the floor and listened to labored breathing. Waves of recollection washed my brain. He knelt before me in an abandoned necropolis and massaged my face with cemetery sod. I shoved stained glass, which had once been a representation of the Christ, into the back of his hand. Dark blood dripped onto our nakedness. He smoothed my mouth with wounded hand.

"Drink this for me," he whispered, cupping my balls with his other hand. "I am the Erection and the Life." Smiling, I tightened my mouth around the ruddy wound and sucked, as he bent low and wound his lips around my aching phallus. Salty elixir spilled into our mouths.

My eyes opened, and I crawled to his hanging form. Rising clumsily to weakened knees, I stretched toward his dry dead hand. Blood had thickened on its new wound. Taking hold of it, I bathed it with tears and kisses. A folded sheet of yellow paper peeked from where it had been stuffed into the pouch that hugged his prick. Releasing his heavy hand, I buried my face into his crotch, drinking in the pungent smell of urine. I took hold of the yellow paper and smoothed it against my face. Its violet letters wavered in the gloom. The words were from his beloved Baudelaire, in Clark Ashton Smith's translation:

"...Despair
Weeps, even as Hope, and dire, despotic Anguish comes
To hang her stifling sable draperies everywhere."

The words had been kissed with bloodstained lips.

I lost it then. Clutching his limbs, I shook with grief, as hopelessness chilled my numb flesh. Misery churned my little soul. It choked my burning throat. Sorrow vomited from my heaving mouth. But his soft hand embraced the scars of my shaven head, and familiar lips pressed against my ear. We fell upon the floor, locked in union, as his mouth bit into my own. I licked the thick blood from his lips, gazed into his eyes, begged for poetry and passion.

"Death is a soul eater," he sighed. "A cherry razorkiss. A fuck dictator. The black sun surgeon cuts into my angst, and poesy pours forth, a mental masturbation. You lick it up, you cow. I am your Venus Psyclone, your sea of stormy love, on which you wreck. I tempest-toss your dick within my fanged Godbox until you beg for clemency."

On and on the words assaulted, as jagged teeth tore into my flesh and drooled into my brain. His rough wet tongue licked my throat, my nipple; it fondled my pulsing heart which he sucked in time to cosmic rhythm. He was the wild beast of romance gone mad. My eyelids flapped open. I watched his whispered wordplay whirl around us in the smoky air. His tattered visage rose before my own, a dim yellow thing wrinkled with woe. The blinking eyes dripped blots of blackness into the scarlet slit that was his mouth. Oh, how that crimson void split with torment. The room was splattered with wet red nightmare.

My bones shuddered. Orgasm stung my phallus. Desperately, I hugged him to me and wound my fingers into his matted hair. His heavy corpse weighed me down with remorseless reality. Dreaming died. Gasping, weeping, I gazed at the broken rope that hung above us. Nasty shadow drifted downward, mocking me until candlelight extinguished.

Cool Mist

Above me loomed that dark abyss, the unknown gulf of night. I remember wandering beneath that realm of ink in search of perfect solitude, hunting for one uninhabited place where I could sit undisturbed and weep for the soul of my young lover, dead by his own hand. Finding my way to the waterfront, which was near to the punk artists' co-op that was my unruly home, I walked in wind that pushed the stink of Puget Sound into my sensitive nostrils. I heard the plash of waves on rocks and approached that liquid song. The somber expanse of water spread before me, seeming like some living thing; reminding me of the mortal elixir that once flowed within my lover's veins, those vital stems into which he pierced a needle and heralded his junky doom. He had mocked my quaint abhorrence of drugs and booze, and I suppose he would laugh to know that I had procured some outlawed absinthe from my Autumn Sister and drank the brew in bitter memory of our love.

Night's chill shook me from my morbid reverie. Shoving hands into pants pockets, I felt the chunk of cheese that I had wrapped in plastic. It had been Todd's habit to feed cheese to the waterfront rats, and I had decided to continue this tradition in his memory. As I began to unwrap the substance, I heard a human sound above the wind and waves. A voice of song. I hesitated, not wanting to meet anyone; but as I listened something in the sound beguiled my senses and seemed to beckon. My boots crunched on pebbles as I trod upon the path that led beyond the rocks and water; and my footfalls must have carried to the singer, for suddenly the song went false. I looked and saw a shape kneeling on the ground, a blanket enshrouding its shoulders. It rocked to and fro, and as I cautiously approached I could detect the soft singing of an esoteric melody.

His small face was that of a child, but his eyes were not young – they gleamed with hostility as they held my own. His dark hair was kept short except for two tufts dyed red and shaped into horns. Spiked dog collars choked his throat. His face contained a kind of ravaged beauty, and it terrified me. There was something in his dark sparkling eyes, a weird kind of crazy rapture that chilled the heart of he who looked upon those slanted orbs.

I knelt a few feet from him. Fearful as I was, I wanted to listen to his tune. The guttural language that he softly uttered was like none I had known; it amazed me that a human mouth could shape such alien words. He turned away from me as I listened and sang to distant water. Trying to think of something to say, I held to him the chunk of cheese. "Care for some? I like feeding the sewer rats, they get so hungry this time of year." I thought I detected a sort of smile. And then he turned his merciless eyes toward mine and opened his mouth in song – a loud wailing sound. I felt stabs of icy terror creep into my flesh. Those weird words of his cacophony filled me with a kind of panic. I leaned upon my hands so as to push myself erect and stalk away.

His singing stopped and he gazed toward the water with frantic eyes. I followed his gaze and at first saw nothing – and then it was there, a patch of mist that floated toward us in dark aether. I thought at first that it reflected moonlight, but then I realized that its odd illumination came from some other, some unknown, source. But what kind of light could form such outlandish hints of hue in the body of dull mist? And what were those colors that writhed obscenely, that shaped themselves outlandishly?

Once more the child-like creature sang. The mist wormed nearer. It pulsed inches from my face, and a wisp of it drifted to me and smoothed itself against my brow. Vision blurred and blood thickened. My skull throbbed with pain. The boy's decadent singing sounded as though it emanated from some other place, some other time. Cold oppression seethed inside my skullspace and spilled toward my heart. Like a drunken thing I tipped and slammed against the ground.

Awareness came as an ache and sense of dull fear. His strong hand helped me find my balance. How unyielding was the hand that held my own. He saddled nearer and pressed his body against my own. I could taste his rancid breath on my lips. And then I noticed, floating above his head, the patch of mist, that monstrous substance that spilled toward and enveloped our conjoined hands. His fingers tightened in their clutching. I could just make out the muted image of our joined hands as the boy opened his mouth in chanting. I watched in horror as the flesh of our locked hands began to ripple and discolor; how it began to shred and dissolve. The mist grew opaque with crimson cloudiness.

Overwhelmed with searing pain, I shut my weeping eyes and tried not to lose consciousness. Lips kissed my hair and pressed against my ear.

"It does get hungry this time of year," a little voice mocked. That was when my mind snapped, and I lost myself within a hysteria of screaming as my companion sang and sang.

Descent into Shadow and Light

I awakened in my windowless tower, to the smell of ancient books and the worms with which they were infested, and swept the pale winged things from where they had nestled in my coiled hair. Pushing the silken coverings from me, I stood and stared at the white sphere of soft illumination that hovered just above my elongated shadow – the sphere that has been, always, my companion. By its light I have devoured the words found within the ancient books, syllables that I could taste when they were spoken. I cannot quite remember how it is I learned the art of reading, but I have a dim semi-recollection of she who danced in my dreams and always held onto a white book, showing me its illuminated leaves and carefully moving her silent lips so that I could comprehend the words that they formed. It was this woman in white who, at the climax of one vision, dissolved into a globe of light that followed me out of slumber and dwelt with me in the lonesome tower; and it was this sphere of radiance that accompanied on my day of resolution, when I determined to vacate the tower and explore the surrounding forest. Thus I departed from the tower room that had been my home for all of memory, stepped down the winding steps of stone and crossed the arched threshold to the floor of silent earth, where all was dark except for the places that were kissed by the glow of the sphere that followed me. I breathed into the icy air and light mist floated through my lips and drifted toward the dark mute trees of the inarticulate forest. Although there was no sound, I imagined that I could detect sly movement behind distant trees, and thought perhaps the pale winged things that nestled in my hair at time of slumber were surreptitiously shadowing my steps. I did not mind – I liked their smooth cold forms when they wove their way into my coiled hair and kissed my scalp.

The dark trees of the endless forest stood like quiet sentinels that watched me on my path, and as the way began to bend and drop toward a lower region I reached out for one nearby trunk, so as to support my balance; but it startled me, as I pressed my palm against the dendroid form, how unsubstantial the creature seemed, as if it could have been an element of a dream through which I wandered. As I contemplated this, the pale sphere that was my attendant shot before me, followed by pale winged things, some of which reached for my hair and tugged me on my way, out of the forest at last and toward a field where slim black stones protruded from the ground. It was only then that I became aware of sensation, as an experience of chilliness enveloped my flesh. The ground on which I stood took on an aspect of solidness, its rough texture unpleasant beneath my naked foot. The sky above me was black as pitch, but as I peered into its vaulted expanse my sphere of light floated just before my face and pressed against my eyes; and then it drifted from me, into the midnight sky, where it transformed into a bloated, fungoid moon that cast decayed light upon the slabs that tilted above the surrounding soil. I touched one slab and tried to read the words that had been etched thereon when the silence of the place was ruptured by a sound with which I was somewhat familiar; for in my tower chamber there had been a collection of bells of various sizes, and I would sometimes entertain myself by lifting them and listening to their clangor. What I now felt on the chilly air and heard within ear's depth was a deep peal, as of from some distant mammoth bell; and wasn't it queer how I could almost see the vibrations of the sound in the air before me and feel them push into my flesh, my eyes, my tingling mouth? And when I followed that sound it was soon accompanied by a lighter trembling of noise – and this, too, I recognized, for one of my possessions in my chamber had been an antique music box that, once wound, played a lilting melody that often ushered me toward slumber. The din that now reverberated in dark air was a similar sound, yet enhanced and weighty.

I followed the enchanting sound and espied the rectangles of golden light that proved to be apertures of a tower that was not unlike mine own. It was from this edifice that the music sounded, music that was a lure and summoned me to climb through one golden aperture, into a bright room. I stepped onto a smooth and polished floor and saw the being that burned beside me, a figure that resembled me in that it had limbs and torso. I saw that the room's illumination came from the creature's upheld hands, which burned with yellow fire. I saw the others of its kind who stood dead still, their flaming hands providing the light by which the chamber's other occupants moved in dance to the music that was performed by figures crowded upon a platform. One of the dancers moved to me, and I marveled at her whiteness, at the artificial wings that had been sewn into her gown, at the touch of her gloved hands as they wove their fingers through my hair. I marveled at the reek that emanated from my new companion, a heavy stench such as had never assaulted my nostrils; and yet, as much as it violated my senses, there was an aspect of it that I found comforting. I was led into the dance and embraced by a fellow in motley who had lost most of the flesh that had once covered his visage, and I laughed at the sense of grim pleasure that emanated from his too-wide grin. Another winged woman in white drifted to me, and I wondered why her feet seemed to float just above the gleaming floor. My heart trembled violently when I beheld the white book that she clasped, the book that was opened to me. I stood, spellbound, as the woman moved the pointed nail of one long talon into my finger, and I nearly fainted at the smell of the dark stuff that began to spill from my punctured flesh. Her hand guided my own to press my wounded finger to the clean white page, and when I took my hand away I saw the insignia of my print upon the shimmering paper.

I was still gazing downward when the white book was removed from me, and thus I saw the image on the floor of polished glass; and I knew that what I was seeing was my own reflection, of which I had read but never witnessed, for there had been neither window nor mirror within my tower chamber. I fell to my knees and touched my hand to my smooth likeness, and I marveled at how I was a thing of iridescent whiteness like unto the sphere of light that had once been my constant companion. I laughed to see how thin the texture of my face had become, thus revealing the skull beneath my mask of flesh. I knew that I would soon join the throng of friendly ghouls that crowded around me, and this knowledge so enchanted me that I raised my face and moaned in ecstasy, at which signal the others gathered 'round me and offered me their ghastly hands, or that which had once been hands. And I hummed in accompaniment to the orchestra's macabre waltz as my compatriots knelt around me and welcomed me within their carrion caress.

Serenade of Starlight

I see the stars have spelt your name in the sky.
-Boy George

I.

We walked arm in arm beneath the humped moon, and I grinned at Stanley's frowning face. He held a piece of paper to an arched streetlamp. "She said it was around here somewhere, at the top of the hill. Curse the woman for not coming with us." I watched him search the crooked street that twisted before us, saw his frown deepen. Pushing him against the ancient brick of the nearest building, I took a pack of cigarettes from his shirt pocket and placed one thin cylinder between his lips. He lit up, and then he coughed.

"This is certainly a charming section of your antique town," I told him. "One can sense within one's soul its agedness. Why, even the hoary darkness seems more venerable than ordinary shade."

Stanley groaned wearily. "Please, Willy, don't wax poetic. It gives me gas when you talk like an Oscar Wilde fairy tale."

Leaning next to him, pressing my back to the cool brick, I gazed toward heaven. "Ah, dear boy, that is not a fairy tale moon. It is the rapacious moon of Salome, casting its edacious light upon the doomed, the dead."

"And the dizzy," he rudely answered; but I shrugged off the implied put-down and took from my pocket a gold compact and tube of lip gloss. Stanley pushed away and began looking into the windows of the buildings that lined the street. "Here," he suddenly shouted, a noise that echoed in the vacant street. I went to him and looked at the small sign above a door. I could hardly make out the dark letters.

"You're certain this is the place?" I asked hesitantly.

"Of course it is. There's Eve's sculpture." I joined him and squinted through the murky glass of the display window. The work in question stood one foot in height. Composed of smooth gray clay, it depicted two nude and hairless creatures standing near an *outré* skeletal tree. The human figures were squat, their bald heads oddly formed. Their facial features were amorphous and amphibian. Each of the tree's sinister branches ended in a serpent's head.

"In the image of Frog created He them," I chuckled. As if in answer to my jest, an eerie wind echoed in the gables above. Gazing through the cloudy window, I thought I could discern a faint illumination within, and shadows that crept through deeper darkness. I went to the door and turned its chilly knob. A fragrance of antiquity, of dust and darkness, wafted toward my painted face.

I entered in, followed by my companion.

We left somber night behind and walked into a different kind of twilight. The glow within the shop was misty and muted; it fell on the shop's items with a kind of ethereal grace. It seemed, this light, as old as were most of the antiquities upon which it rested. It was warm and primordial on my eyes. How oddly it draped my tingling flesh. My lungs breathed it in, deeply, and I imagined that I could taste dead aeons of forgotten time.

"I'm gonna look around. If I find any cool jewelry, I'll howl," Stanley told me, and I raised my hand in regal reply. I moved past pillars of brittle books and piles of furniture, ran my fingers across the dust that covered a brass lamp and smoothed the residue of dust into my mauve hair. I looked at Stanley, who stood some little distance from me examining a piece of Egyptian statuary. Were we alone is this forlorn place? Was there no proprietor to deplete us of our gold? I moved past a wall of faded photographs, watched by a myriad of dead eyes.

Coming on a small alcove, I stepped within it and stood before a curious display, gasping in delight at the armlets of white gold that sat on beds of purple velvet. It was the necklace of black pearls that made me shout. It took no especial sensitivity to beauty to fully appreciate their unearthly splendor. How queerly they caught the obscure light of the little room, to catch and transpose it to a different order of spectrum. I felt its weird reflection on my eyes, felt it sink beneath those jellied orbs and find my brain. Taking my eyes from the necklace, I studied the statuette that sat on a brick of obsidian glass. The thing was an image of some wild monster of nightmare, a winged mammoth that squatted on humanoid legs, whose pulpy tentacle face wore an aspect of age-old evil. How strange, that this entity seemed vaguely familiar, like something witnessed in some pocket of forgotten memory.

"Entrancing, isn't he?"

I turned and looked at the handsome young man who stood near me. I had a kinky thing for those skinhead types, and he was a beauty, with an aura that hinted of danger. I gazed into his aqua eyes.

"As entrancing as sin," I simpered. "He seems to be awaiting some secret thing."

"Perhaps he waits for you." He reached toward a shelf that had been built into the wall and took from it a large pale seashell. How fondly he held it, how tenderly he put its cavity to my ear. "What do you hear?"

"An echo that mocks the sound of waves on sand," I replied quickly; then paused as another sound, a dim vibration of humming, crept into my ear. I frowned, and the sound faded. Perhaps it had been naught but imagination. I smiled as the young man studied my face with fascinating eyes; and then I felt a taint of unease as his wide eyes seemed to darken. I turned to look again at the string of black pearls.

"You seem hypnotized by that necklace."

"It's exactly what I'm looking for. I'm going to a ball and need a bit of sparkle, something simple yet stylish. Those onyx gems would do perfectly. But I sense that they are not available."

"They're not for sale, this case is for display only; but I could loan them to you."

"My dear boy, you can't be serious. You know nothing of me."

Stepping nearer, he spoke with soft low voice. "I know that you're a creature of fancy, a dreamer and a poet. Wings of vision have brushed your brain. You've seen things in slumber that you but vaguely remember, hazy things that fill you with fanciful fear and curious longing. No matter the society you find yourself in, you are always an outsider."

I arched an eyebrow. With whom had this gentleman been talking? "We've met before?"

"Not in the waking world," was his enigmatic reply. His thick lips formed an esoteric smile. Everything about him seemed suddenly familiar, yet strangely so. I watched his hands reach for the necklace, and quaked slightly as he walked behind me and placed the string of pearls around my throat. His solid body, with its odd sweetly sour aroma, leaned heavily against mine as he fastened a clasp. How cold were the hands that touched my skin, how colder still the onyx gems.

"Will?" Stanley entered the alcove and grimaced at the scene before him. I felt deliciously wicked.

"What do you think, my dear?" I asked, fingering the pearls.

"Oh, very nice. How clever of you to find a color that matches your soul."

"Do they make me look monarchal?"

"Every inch a queen. All you need now is a crown."

"Excuse me, gentlemen," whispered the young proprietor, who vanished for a long moment in which Stanley gave me a naughty look, which I superbly ignored. When the young man returned, I gasped in wonder at the object in his hands. "It's been in my family for generations. As you can see, it's composed of the same material as the other items. You'll notice an identical pictorial motif, those curious aquatic creatures." He spoke this in his low, entrancing voice, never taking his eyes from me. I sensed that his every word was pregnant with hidden meaning that I was somehow supposed to comprehend; but what he was trying to communicate I could not fathom, despite the urgency in his eyes and voice.

I reached for the tiara of white gold, shivered at the chilliness of its surface, studied intently its bizarre motifs. I fancied that I had witnessed their likenesses before, in that elusive pocket of memory that had begun to beckon in my brain. I brought the diadem to my dome.

"It must have gotten damaged in shipping," said Stanley. "Look at how it's bent. It'll never fit." He proved correct; and yet, as I placed the magnificent work upon my head I was overwhelmed with uncanny sensation. It was similar to what I felt when entering my grandmother's old house. Certain smells and shapes brought to vivid life long-buried memories, smells and tastes. As the golden tiara pressed against my head, I sensed things both alien and familiar. Oh, how its cold metal seemed to sink beneath my temple and chill my brain. Shutting eyes, I seemed to hear once more the echo of song that I had detected when the seashell had been placed against my ear. Softly, I hummed the semi-melody. I sensed the movement of forceful water and swayed to ebb and flow. I tilted and began to fall.

He held me in strong arms, and his unblinking eyes seemed triumphant. Removing myself from his embrace, I took the thing of gold from my head and studied its eccentric shape. Certainly, the large and curiously irregular periphery seemed intended for a head of freakish design. However, the rim did not, as Stanley had suggested, appear bent or damaged – its metal was too perfectly smooth, unmarred in any way. I turned to the silent fellow and handed him the tiara, then pulled out my wallet, from which I took my photo I.D. and a twenty-dollar bill. "This is to assure my return of your wonderful necklace. Stanley, this magnificent young fellow is allowing me to borrow these onyx gems for the ball. Isn't he divine?"

The young man took my hand and kissed it, then waved away my offering. "My payment is the joy of seeing you smile, and knowing that my grandmother's pearls will adorn a creature of exceptional beauty. Wear them to your ball, and then return. I'll be here, awaiting you."

I gazed into those blue eyes that seemed to contain some wisdom of the ages. I could look into their beauty forever. I could not pull myself away. Grabbing my sleeve, Stanley muttered thanks and dragged me to the door.

II.

Waves of incoherent sound washed over me. He held the large sea conch in his steady hand. As I beheld its circular aperture, I felt myself fall into its swirling obscurity and become one with cryptic darkness. Around me throbbed the sound of storm, of water, of electric air. Curling shadow stalked my soul, a blackness I could taste. The ebb and flow of sound became a riot of vociferation; and underneath that noise

I heard echoed one fantastic name:

Y'ha-nthlei.

I whispered the strange, the beautiful word as his thick lips pressed against my throat. Not closing my eyes, I stared steadfastly at the idol of chiseled stone that wavered in black space, the texture of which glistened, the eyes of which gleamed wetly. His tongue at my throat played with the pearls against my neck, and as he kissed those midnight gems they broke free and dropped into his hand. Madly, I laughed as he pitched them into sky, and I howled as they blossomed like aphotic blooms in some sunken city; a city of pillars, of gigantic steps that led to some monolithic crypt. I convulsed with ecstasy as a liquid voice from beyond the sculptured mass of door called my name.

"Willy?"

I awakened to the loveliest pair of eyes I had ever seen. Indeed, the entire face was composed of breathtaking beauty; not merely the loveliness of youth, but rather a radiance that seemed ageless. She brushed her auburn hair from the smooth and perfect complexion of her face and smiled with full rose-tinted lips.

"You asked me to wake you up before I left for the studio."

Wearily, I stirred beneath the bedclothes. "Ah, yes, darling. What time *is* it?"

"Three in the afternoon. Fucking Stanley had you out all night. Whatever were you two about?"

"Well, he had to see *The Fags* reunion gig, that punk band whose singer was one of the first scene freaks to die of AIDS. Then he led me in search of your friend's shop." I threw to her a significant look. Playfully, she licked her lips.

"What'd you think of Ian?"

"Is that his name? I never asked. My child, he made me so dizzy I nearly swooned. In fact, I *did* swoon! Actually, it was rather peculiar, for I seemed to almost remember him from somewhere…"

"From your dreams, perhaps."

"My wet dreams, certainly. And speaking of liquid dreams, I had a most peculiar one about your curious piece of art."

"Really, you've been dreaming about *The Vault of Time*? I'm flattered."

"What exactly did it represent, some sacrilegious motif?"

She climbed into bed with me and pressed her bosom to my chest. "The odd fact is," she whispered, her face close to mine, " it's something I saw in recurring dream, a vision I had during an organic high."

"My dear – narcotics!"

"Purely organic, bitch. Don't be such a prude. If you're a good girl I'll share with you before you leave our old town and return to mad city life." I batted my eyes at her, then pressed my hand against a sudden pain that pierced my head. "What?"

"My head feels rather queer, dear. Have you any aspirin?" She took my head into her hands and softly stroked. In her low and lovely voice she hummed a tune that seemed familiar. My flesh prickled. I gazed into her eyes, those golden eyes flecked with green and blue. Bending to her, I bit her lower lip and began to unbutton her blouse. Moving her mouth to my ear, she breathed into it her strange song. I fingered the dark nipples of her breasts and imagined that I could feel my skull expand with shifting shape, with delicious pain. Her fingers combed my flowing hair. Shutting eyes, I dreamed of Ian, and suddenly it was his hand that fondled me. I watched his other hand twist the necklace that I wore until it broke. Catching the pearls that spilled into his hand, he tossed them above us, and I watched them form a cluster of midnight stars that glimmered as darkly as an idol's jeweled eyes. Cosmic wind rose in melody, accompanying the song that was blown into my ears by hungry mouth. It was a song to chill starlight, and as I listened I saw the dead stars crawl across the sky and form an elder sign.

"I'll see you tonight," Eve whispered. I smiled but did not open my eyes. Lost is trance, I sank into bed. When again I woke, the light of day had departed. Staggering into the bathroom, I washed my numb face. My head ached, and as I looked at my reflection I saw a curious thing. My face seemed subtly altered, as did my dome. I lifted a strand of yellow hair, loathing the feel of it, the sickly color of it. Searching Eve's toiletries, I found the razor. How cool it felt against my scalp. My skull still ached with dull pain, my eyesight was blurred, but I did not care. I filled my hands with warm water and washed it over my newly-shaven head. I dried my dome and studied it in the glass. How wonderful it felt. Leaning nearer to the mirror, I studied the shape of my altered eyes.

Her reflection joined mine. She smoothed powder over my scalp, a strangely scented substance. "I've been waiting a long time for this moment. I suspected that you were linked, ever since you first came to visit staid old Stanley. It's fantastic how we sometimes know our own. Your transition is occurring more quickly than mine, thanks to Ian's art. It's apparent in my eyes alone, which are changing in color and shape. But I've too much bloody human in my genes. Ian tells me to be patient, because he says we have all time. He's been waiting for you, dreaming of you. It's cosmic fate, all of it!"

"Honey, whatever are you babbling about?"

"We share a genetic history, William. We are of the Deep. You're confused, I know, but sensations are swimming to your cells and awakening memory. Ian has told me much that I can't comprehend. He's taken me to Innsmouth, where once we thrived."

"And how did he know that you are of this culture, or whatever it is of which we are a part?"

"Because of my art. And because of where we first met. Let me show you the place, now. " And so she dressed me and drove us to a derelict section of the ancient town. I could smell the nearby sea as she walked me through what had once been a park, and as we approached an alcove I could hear the sound of falling water. I beheld the tilted columns that composed a fountain, where water trickled from apertures in the stone. Beyond the dripping columns was a wall of water. Slipping off her shoes, and indicating that I should do likewise, Eve led me into the shallow pool. As we passed beneath the columns I noticed that upon their surface had been chiseled symbols that were somehow familiar.

She stopped before the granite wall and watched its flow of water. "This is where I met Ian, when I first came to this antique town. I came here and felt – I don't know, a sense of destiny. I had been sculpting for a few years, had a sketchbook filled with dream imagery. You can imagine how stunned I was to find this place, for it corresponded to something I had beheld in recurring dream. It was built in the spring of 1925, at a time when artists and lunatics around the world shared a singular vision: of a city beneath the sea, of the slumbering titan housed therein."

I walked toward the wall and let its liquid flow wash over my hand. Shutting eyes, I saw the face that had been carved upon the surface that I touched. I saw it as living entity. I felt my knees bend in supplication. Oh, my head, how it writhed with numbing pain. I felt my skull stretch with shaping. Kneeling beside me, Eve kissed my throat. I looked past her, to where Ian stood watching us. How magnificent he looked against the background of dark sky and dim starlight. Ah, those cosmic gems, those stars that moved so as to form archaic cosmic symbols.

Ian reached into his shoulder bag and brought out the tiara of white gold. I trembled as he placed it on my head. It was a perfect fit.

Graffito Flow

We stood, Philippe Amarinth and I, in a gallery, looking at renditions of the Christ. I could tell from my friend's expression that he had no especial admiration for the artwork. Philippe was a connoisseur of death imagery, and he was hoping to find at this particular show a feast of sacred gloom. I turned to gaze at him as he laughed out loud while gawking at one rather shabby attempt at art.

"Here we have the Christ as some sort of Immaculate Masturbator. Really, that heart with its tawdry crown of thrones should be a phallus. Bah! Is that camp expression the face of one who has suffered ultimate indignation and torment? Is there any shadow of awful extinction, any trace of the profound poetry of the Lord's magnificent sacrifice?"

His questions did not seek for answers from myself, and so I remained silent. Leaving the blue light of the main gallery we entered a room that was bathed in a crimson hue. The walls were painted red, and upon one surface there was a mess of painted lines and squiggles, looking as if some infant had gone wild with a can of spray paint. I chuckled at this sorry attempt at art and turned to leave but then I saw my companion's face, the eyes from which a teardrop gently fell.

"This is amazing," he whispered, holding up a hand as if to reach for some sacred object. "Don't you see it, dear boy? Look again."

Sighing, I turned and gazed at the mess on the wall; and slowly I began to discern a design, an image. My friend leaned near me and whispered in my ear.

"Yes, the more deeply one looks, the more he reveals himself. That madness of dripping circles becomes the lowered head, a head weighed by the sins of the world. And those sprays on either side, you see, are nothing less than the outstretched arms of crucifixion. It is almost nothing more than symbolic, and yet he is there in all of his tragic glory. Those drips—you see how they form into pellets of blood? My god—my god."

And then he shuddered—from ecstasy or horror I could not tell— and I followed as he turned and fled from that place, rushing through the main gallery and finding our way outside. Stopping to rest against a wall, Philippe placed an Egyptian cigarette into his mouth and lit up, ignoring my soft coughing and disapproving frown. It was twilight, and the full moon, tainted orange, sat low and large in the semi-darkness.

Taking one final puff, my friend flicked his cigarette into the gutter, linked his arm with mine, and led me strolling down the sidewalk. "Do you find it sad, Russell, the lack of originality in today's culture, the lack of authenticity? Now, that gallery is reputed to be the showplace of radical Bohemian artwork, but did you see anything really daring? The clientele of cool seem lost in some kind of time warp. Did you notice that pale young child holding tightly to his second-hand copy of Kerouac and dressed in black? What a sad cliché. What a poverty of poetical imagination. The entire scene, from the artists to their art, is merely a copy of something else. That's why I like you, dear boy."

"You like me because I'm very young and very ugly."

"Yes, I see the beauty in your bestial face, the wonder dancing in your wild green eyes. And I see your unaffected devotion to death, and to its manifestations. You were the first child that I ever picked up in a cemetery. I was instantly attracted to your oddness, an allurement that has made you such a hit in that freak show you travel with."

"I find a peacefulness in places of death, and strange joy in images of the tomb. But I have to admit that that spray painting or whatever the hell it was we saw tonight got to me."

"Yes, it was unique. That's what I look for in art, yet seldom find. I saw it in Pilon's tomb for Henry II and his Catherine, in those unpretentious figures of their nude corpses, those recumbent marble *gisants*. I saw it in Friedrich's *Abbey in an Oak Forest,* a work that is the epitome of eternal and melancholy extinction. It's been compared to Ruisdael's *Jewish Cemetery,* but there's no comparison. Ruisdael is all abundant movement, the wind in the trees, the rolling clouds pregnant with electrical life. In Friedrich there is nought but dry and lonely death."

We had continued our stroll, and I saw that we were walking down Half Moon Street, on the deserted edge of the downtown area. The full moon was a little higher in the sky, and far more pale. Finally, we reached the end of pavement, pausing before a field of dirt. A figure sat some distance from us, bent and digging with one finger in the ground. The silent night was haunted by her low, uncanny singing.

We slowly approached her, and my friend leaned to me so as to whisper, "She draws in the dirt, like Christ. Perhaps she is full of parables." When we were three feet from her, Phillipe squatted and smiled. "Good Madonna, we have come to learn our future."

She had not stopped her soft low humming. Glancing at my companion for one moment, she graced him with an uncanny smile, then began to move her finger in the dirt. Philippe's expression became very serious as he watched the creation of her art, and I moved closer so as to see the moonlit portrait that formed beneath the creature's moving hand. I gasped at the likeness of the portrait: it was my friend's face, formed in simple lines; and yet it was devoid of life. It could have been a death's mask made of dirt. Philippe's breath issued heavily from his moving mouth. Suddenly, he thrust his hand onto the ground and wiped the face away, then reached into a pocket and brought out a soiled handful of cash, which he tossed onto the ruined portrait. The woman stopped her humming, gazed at my friend's face, reached for that face with a hand that moved its rough flesh across Philippe's smooth skin.

She held that hand to the full moon, then offered a ringed finger to the man before her. Tenderly, he moved the scarab ring from her claw and touched it to his lips, then pulled it onto his finger.

I followed him as he rose and walked away, strolling to an alley between what looked like two abandoned factories. Leaning against the old brick of one building, he looked at his new ring for a little while, then reached into a pocket and produced a cigarette. "You look a bit dashed, dear boy," he informed me. "You are like so many youngsters I have known, who profess a romantic and aesthetic appreciation of death, but who become depressed at the idea of their own extinction. I am guessing that that is the origin of your long face and sober expression. But look around you, at this man-made world. How wonderful it will be to escape it, to lie undisturbed in our porphyry tombs, couched in quietude."

"If death is the absolute end . . ."

"Is that what's bothering you? Yes, the idea of life after death is depressing. What could be more damnable than eternal life? But I don't believe in anything beyond the grave, and that is why death's imagery and symbolism is of such comfort. Come, let us walk into this alley and escape the moon."

I had expected, as we entered the alleyway, to be assaulted by the stench of hobo piss, but the only scent that assailed my nostrils was the odor of my companion's exotic cigarette. I watched as the smoke he emitted sailed upward, out of semi-darkness and into dim moonlight, as from the area we had but just vacated there came the sound of low and distant singing, a sound that, queerly, did not seem to be for us but rather an offering to unknown gods.

We slowly walked between what seemed to be very old brick factories, and I was caught by a sense of isolation that I had never known before. The place seemed unwholesomely lonely. Moonlight filtered down to illuminate one slender portion of the alley, shining on a strange lump of what turned out to be discarded clothing. I stepped closer so to examine the bundle of garments and then reached for a shard of shattered wine glass that littered the ground. Rising, I held the shard to moonlight, admiring how its amber surface caught the dead and distant light. And that was when I noticed the writing on the wall.

"What the devil . . .?" Philippe whispered, gazing at the graffiti. "Good Jesu, it looks like some kind of outlandish foreign alphabet, until you make out the figure in the carpet, if I may be allowed a reference to my favorite author. Look, don't you see it, that circle there, it could be a head heavily bowed with the suffering of the world. And those outstretched squiggles—how similar to that other thing we saw in the gallery tonight. But to find it in this desolate place . . ."

I watched as he walked to it and placed a hand upon its surface. Hypnotically, I moved just behind him, listening to his heavy breathing as he sucked in one final puff on his fag and then flicked the butt away. I felt my face flush with outrage; for this seemed a holy place, a sacred ground, and for him to litter it with such nonchalance filled me with sudden fury.

"Look," he whispered, "you can just make it out in this remarkable half-light: a face of some kind, there, hideously stretched and distorted, yet wearing still an expression of bewildered fear and torment. It creeps my flesh, Russell. I've never seen anything like it." Turning to face me, he heavily leaned against the pattern on the wall, raising his face to the iris-blue sky of early twilight, lifting his arms until he looked like some well-fed parody of Crucifixion.

I leaned toward him and kissed his mouth. "Let me complete the picture," I whispered, then brought the shard of glass to one of his hands, over which I quickly ran the edge of broken glass. He hissed in surprise and pain, and then he smiled and called me a perverse child, leaning to me so as to touch his lips once more to mine. I evaded his kiss and slowly ran the dirty shard over the back of his other hand. Flesh parted, and his mortal liquid dripped onto the pattern on the wall.

I knelt before him and brought my prayerful hands together, those hands that were slightly stained by the residue of blood that smeared the shard of glass I held. He foolishly smiled at me, basking in what he took to be my adoration. I could see from his smug smile that to be worshipped was a thing he felt worthy of. But it was not Philippe Amarinth that I so piously venerated, but rather that pattern on the wall, that outré graffiti that began to subtly ripple and expand. He, the vain fellow, could not see it with his back to the wall, how his blood had not spilled onto the ground but rather was absorbed by the alien substance that hungrily moved behind my companion.

I watched, entranced, as Philippe suddenly frowned, as he finally turned to look at his hand, that pale white glove of flesh that withered and grew flat, that conjoined with the moving pattern it had pressed against. I watched as the scarab ring fell from the changing flesh, landing with a dull thud onto the bundle of discarded clothing. I watched his wonderful expression of bewildered fear as a cloud of mauve mist began to issue from the moving thing, that thing that sucked the fellow's flesh inexorably into it. I watched as they rose together along the wall, flowed along the wall so as to reach a place of bright moonlight, and I smiled at the almost clownish way that Philippe's clothing fell as a heap onto the alleyway.

They moved, the alien thing and its new victim, and still I could see a semblance of my friend's face, flattened and stretched, with lunar beams burning in what remained of eyes. Finally, I lowered my gaze, reached for the scarab ring, and slipped it onto a bloodstained hand.

From somewhere in the distance, a madwoman raised her voice in eerie song.

Depths of Dreams and Madness

I.

"Open your eyes, Simon. I need to capture their allure."

Simon Gregory Williams stirred in his chair, opened his eyes and frowned at the fellow who sat before him. The artist gazed with keen interest at Simon's face, and then he touched brush to canvas and continued working his exceptional art. Simon, a little bored, pressed his lips together and sighed a strange melody that stirred the particles that drifted, barely discernable, in the candlelit air. The artist stopped working for a moment so as to watch those minute specs that floated all around them and saw how they caught the candlelight and shimmered with curious shades of green and gold and violet; and this reminded him of similar flecks of color that shimmered in the silver eyes of his host.

"Why have you stopped working?" The beast's frown had deepened. "Do you grow fatigued? Have you need to stretch your human limbs?"

"I was merely listening to your tune."

Simon smiled. "A curious little ditty, is it not? I like the way it stirs the chemistry of earthly elements. Observe." Reaching into an inside pocket of his jacket, he produced a thin black flute, which he pressed to his lips and began to play, performing once more the air he had whistled. Now the sound was bold and wove around them, and the artist shivered as he watched the way the candle's flame darkened and expanded, at the way the shadows in the room began to merge and bend. He watched one rising patch of shadow that shaped itself before him as a bestial thing that opened wide its jaws, and he dropped his brush as that shadow-snout heaved a spectral howl. "Amusing, isn't it?"

The mortal bent to retrieve his brush. "It's a curious art, certainly."

Simon shrugged. "An art nonetheless. I summon shadows, as you do with you palette."

"I summon actuality, Simon – without its mask. I'm a realist. I summon up the past, a thing that the present folk of 1926 don't want to think about. They're all afraid of the past, yet they don't know why."

"They love the sparkle of their neoteric toys. Just as you love what you fancy are the shadows of the past; but yours is merely the paltry human past, a negligible thing. There are far elder things than the ghouls you bring to life, again and again. What a curious *idée fixe*, and how it dominates your vision."

"I have no vision or philosophy as an artist. As I just told you, I'm a realist – I paint what I see, the things I locate."

"And give to them your queer interpretation. That is the secret of your art."

"It's a queer old world, Simon. My secret, as you call it, comes from knowing where to look for inspiration. I dig into the depths of nature and find her hidden gems of horror. I capture the potency of unclean things unearthed, but I allow them to keep much of their mystique. I show a little, and suggest a lot."

"Nonsense, there is far more than suggestion in that delightful painting you've named 'The Lesson,' wherein a child is taught to feast with fiends. It's remarkably blunt, that one. And it shews another of your manias – the idea of the changeling."

The artist's expression altered as his eyes seemed to look inward, and Simon noticed how both face and eyes had darkened. "It's an interesting idea, the notion of secret exchange, of a thing not quite human being raised among common folk. When would such a child begin to suspect her alien nature, and what would trigger such suspicion? It might be dreams of sunken things, or memories of unnatural hungers. It might be something secretly revealed in the reflection on a mirror. There would be weird instincts that guide the misfit to the hidden spaces of the world, the realms of shadow that may prove illuminating. There may be talents that are expressed in such a manner that, in time, those who were comrades fade away in fear. For it wouldn't be a quality that one can hide forever from the world. People would begin to suspect. There must be a kind of ancestral connection between the human and the Other, an aspect that eventually arouses suspicion."

"Yes," Simon responded. "And such mistrust can lead to crimes against the Other, as your Salem ancestor discovered when they swung her on Gallows Hill with Cotton Mather looking on. They murdered her because of her books, you told me."

"Most of which they burned. But some few were hidden well, and they were not destroyed. I've brought one of them with me, to give you as a gift."

The beast's eyes sparkled. "Indeed?" He watched as the artist reached down to the satchel on the floor next to his chair, out of which he pulled an oblong object that was wrapped in purple silk. Simon's nostrils quivered at the scent of ancient alchemy. He watched as the silk was removed, and then he knew instantly what the other held. "Ah yes, the thing of legend. I knew of the vague rumor that credited the preservation of a sixteenth-century Greek text to a clan of Salem witches. 'Tis well preserved. Have you read it?"

"I've looked it over. I haven't inherited an interest in magick. Knowing of your obsession, I thought to give you this so that you can add it to your pile in the tower. You look satisfied."

"I am more than satisfied, dear Pickman. I didn't hope that it had survived. There was a curious burning of a certain Salem man's library, one that contained the Greek translation of Theodorus Philetas of Constantinople. There are far more translations of *Al Azif* than has been alleged by so-called experts, but they are often incomplete or incompetent. The original Arabic text has been forever lost, alas. I've tried to commune with the shade of its author, but every trace of his psyche has been sipped into the void by the devils he raised up. This is a wonderful gift, and I thank you. Are we finished for the night?"

The artist grinned – his friend was anxious to investigate his treasure. "I suppose so," he replied as he stood and stretched. "It's nearly done."

Simon rose, book in hand, and went to look at the painted image.

151

"Ah, excellent. Faces are your forte, absolutely. You have captured to perfection my diabolic nature."

"It's not difficult to depict something so evident," the artist chuckled. "You interest me greatly, you know – I find your nature intriguing."

At this the beast laughed outloud. "I sensed your fascination when I attended your last show in Boston. What a spectacle that was! How your canvases outraged the unimaginative rabble. I think you lost your final patron because of that exhibition – although you still receive a trivial imbursement from your poor father. Or do you? How stalwart he stood, at that shocking presentation of some of your most powerful work, knowing full well the scandal you had scored. That show was a kind of suicide, and I greatly admired your grim audacity. I knew at once that you would be the ideal artist to paint my portrait, and thus I offered you that outlandish sum and brought you here. But it was not simply the smell of capital that caught your interest – you were immediately captivated by my face. Unlike others of my kind, I do not deign to disguise my nature while traversing outside Sesqua Valley. I delight in the displeasure that my features arouse. They certainly stimulated you, and I know why – you think that I fit in with your idea of the changeling, your rich obsession. You are awestruck by the link between that which is human and that which is Other. This link is your continual artistic motif. I recognized it at once when first I beheld one of your canvases. I was certain that in finding you I had found the fellow who could paint me as I am. This canvas proves me correct. It's absolutely accurate."

Simon squinted his eyes as he continued. "But you have captivated as well. You are so interesting. I've seen photos of you, from earlier exhibitions, in newspapers and such, and I find it intriguing how you have altered. How full of hint, the way you're beginning to resemble your work, like an interesting 'take' on Wilde's witticism about nature aping art. Your flesh has darkened, and its very texture has altered so as to bear a resemblance to the hide of your ghouls. Your features have transformed – your mouth is wider than is natural, your teeth more square. Your nose has flattened and expanded. And your jade eyes – were they not brown for most of your life? And your odor. . ." Simon's nostrils flared as he tilted nearer to the artist and inhaled. "You reek of the debris of tombs, of cemetery sod. And not only this – your dreams have been infected, as I discovered when you took your little nap. A detritus of nightmare clings to your psyche, and tatters of lurid visions cling to your little brain. You have wallowed in pits of airy sewage and brought its offal with you to this mortal clime. I smell it absolutely, this rot of dreaming. It is an art some of us possess, to enter human dreaming and coax its course. In dream you have tried to ascertain your secrecy of origin. You try to stir memory, but all you really rouse are nebulous shadows that may have linkage to your past."

"You may be right," the artist whispered. "My favorite place on earth is Copp's Hill Burying Ground, in Boston. There are shadows in the North End that are like none others – an elder darkness. I have a private studio there, where I keep the canvases on which I've set my fancy free." Grimly, he laughed. "God, if those fools thought my last show was scandalous – they've no idea! It is there, in that sequestered studio, where I feel most at home. It's there that I smell most forcibly the past, in all its peculiar splendor. I let the shadow of old time coat my eyes and churn my brain. I let it influence my work, yet subtly. People rarely notice those little touches, they're too fixated on the faces of my fiends and the ancestral recall thus aroused. But they're there – behind the devilish portraits: the spectres of a dead and buried age, revealed in blurred images of brick edifices, old stone, decayed woodwork, another era that I artistically evoke. A potent past. The past, the past – it's all there is!"

"There are, however, other evocations – beyond dimensional time. And there are a myriad of dreams. I sensed other visions churning in your skull – dreams of alien landscape and one who awaits you within strange shadow." He looked lovingly at the book he held. "This book is a connotation of the potency of dreaming."

"And to such things I now leave you, Simon. My work here is finished for the nonce. Sweet dreams, sir."

Simon opened the book and ran tapered fingers across one page. "No, no," he whispered, "I never dream." But his words went unheeded, for he was alone in his little room.

II.

(From the Journal of Richard Upton Pickman)

I returned to my spacious room above the curio shop and sat in fabulous darkness where I brooded on my plight. The situation at home had become precarious, with even my father refusing to see me in the end. I suppose he fancied that I had become enslaved by narcotics and that they had altered my very being. He was a fool not to realize the facts – for he had always treated me like I was something strange and unwanted, and this suggested that he knew or suspected something about my origin, my smuggle into his household. We had had one final fight about my mother – I demanded to be told about her, about why she had vanished when I was a boy. I knew instinctively that she had held the key to my mystery of hatching into this hateful world. She has visited me, often, in my queerest dreams, and with each visit she looked a little altered. Often she was accompanied by two silent creatures, winged things with flesh as black as midnight, fiends without faces. The curious thing was that when I looked into the mirror upon awakening, I saw that my mug was changing in a way that matched my mother's alteration in my dreams. I am now much distorted. Just now, returning from Simon's hovel in the woods, I noticed that I can no long walk like I used to, and I can't stand erect. I slump forward, and something about my pelvis has so altered that I lope in a way that isn't natural. Lately I've noticed the alteration of my hands, and this has really displeased me, because I'm afraid it will affect the way I paint; for my mitts have enlarged, and my nails are strong and square. No matter, I can still hold a brush as well as ever, and my work on Simon's portrait is nearly done. As is this final work that I am completing in this room – this portrait of the artist as a fiend, this artistic investigation of what has become my countenance. This place is cozy, and I like that it still has an acetylene gas outfit as its light source rather than modern electricity – just like my studio in the North End. I brought one of my own lanterns from the studio, so I am with familiar things that help give me a sense of being home.

Of course, this valley could never be my home. I protested to

Simon that I need a sense of the past in which to dwell – the ancient buildings and lanes and secrets of New England. He scoffed at me and said that such things were modern compared to the agedness of this valley and its forest. He said that the secrets of antique Boston, which were merely a construct of mankind, could not compare to the enigmas of this place. Bah. I'll admit that Sesqua Valley is rather weird. I don't like the smell of the air – it has a cloying sweetness that sticks inside my throat. And there isn't anything sinister, that I can perceive, in the fresh green shadows of the woods. I long to return home, however lonesome Boston has become. The last of my friends dropped me after that final exhibition – but I had a hunch that they would; and, really, that was part of my intention, to shock the community by finally showing some of my secret canvases, the things I had until then kept sequestered in my North End studio. Roberta suspected the kind of reception the paintings would have, which is why she allowed me to display them in her gallery. She prides herself on being Bohemian, although most of her pals are merely surrealists. Well, it tickled her to display my canvases, and I delighted in the demonstrations of shock and dismay, which indeed helped to fuel my hatred for humanity.

Simon was something unsuspected, and at first I loathed his keen interest. But his suggestion of a temporary escape from everything, in this remote corner of the world, interested me. And, let's face it – the paintings no longer sell. So I packed some gear and drove us up here in my jalopy, and that in itself felt rather wonderful, the thrill of sudden flight, the fun idea of my mysterious evaporation from the Boston scene, and the long drive itself, through unfamiliar country. I relished it. Simon proved an amusing companion, and I loved the reaction to his persona when we stopped at the motel. He laughed when I called him 'beast' and said that I was not the first to do so. I don't quite understand what's wrong with his face. It doesn't seem like birth defect, but rather some kind of racial thing. And I've noticed, in the small time I've been in town, others who share this queer hereditary stain, so it must be some inbred thing associated with this place. Rather like one finds in the clans of Innsmouth. I love painting him, as it gives me an excuse to *study* his freakishness. There is indeed something purely bestial in his cruel features. At times his mug reminds me of a wolf, or a frog. It's his eyes that absolutely captivate, with their silver sheen, like pale nickel; and I've noticed, in certain light, a grouping of queerly colored particles floating on the surface of his eyes. And, yes, as I mentioned above – they are malicious eyes, malignant in a haughty sort of way. You get the idea that he is plotting on how best to hurt you.

I had Roberta use my camera to take a series of snaps of myself, close up, just my face. I like working from photographs. I like the way they can reveal things that mirrors cannot, how things are captured, subtly. I'm using them to work on my final . . . *Why* I insist on thinking of this self-portrait as my *final* work I cannot fathom, but the word comes continually to mind. Maybe it's just a hunch that my days as an artist in Boston are at an end.

Simon mentioned that a group of aesthetic folk meet at some kind of arty club or saloon in town tonight, and he thought it might amuse me to comingle. I doubt it, but what the hell, might as well see what the locals are like. It's weird and rather stupid, to have grown so hateful of humanity, and yet to fight against a kind of cosmic lonesomeness. The mind of man – who can comprehend it? Mine remains a mystery. Take your sketchpad, Richard. Some of the folks you've seen share Simon's curious features, although none as outlandish as his own. You may find a slew of future portraits among the happy villagers.

III.

It was not a lengthy walk from his room to the hostelry where the locals congregated, but the artist took his time in strolling to the place. It was true that this valley town did not have those charms that had so captivated him in Boston, that sense of hoary past; and yet Sesqua Town had her own special appeal – that of an old and isolated haunt. The sidewalks, for example, were made of planks of solid wood, and none of the roads were paved. So yes, there was a feeling of the past in this place, but not such a one as could compare to that of New England. What Sesqua Valley did suggest was the timelessness of nature – and this was something that Boston, with its bricks and warehouses and cobblestone lanes, lacked. New England's past was that of man – this valley's agelessness was outside human design. He stopped in his walking to look at the titanic twin-peaked mountain, the white stone of which seemed to soak in a quality of the light that shone from the quarter moon, reflecting that light on its shimmering surface of majestic rock. The artist was utterly captivated by that mountain, for he had never seen such peaks, lean and curved and rising over the mountain at great height, resembling to imaginative souls fantastic wings extending from a daemon's shoulders.

A wind arose and pushed against his eyes, and as he continued to gaze at the mountain the artist was suddenly overwhelmed with eerie sensation. He thought that he could detect within the wind a subtle sound, like a distant siren song that would enchant him toward devastation. An element of wind seemed to sink inside the surface of his eyes and alter their perception, and he swore that the colossal mountain moved, lazily, and stretched its peaks. He was overwhelmed with an ache to march to that mountain and climb so as to sing beneath the shadows of those peaks. Richard began to move toward the thing of shimmering stone, until a hand clutched at his arm and turned him around. Protesting, he tried to shake free of the fellow and peer toward the peaks once more, but his sudden companion would not allow him to do so.

"No, you don't want to stare at that white stone. Ignore its call. You're the artist everyone has been chattering about, the beast's new amigo?"

Richard shook his head as if to clear it, and then he extended his hand, which was clasped by the stranger. "Richard Pickman, of Boston. Yes, Simon lured me here to paint his portrait."

The fellow moved a little nearer, and the artist curled his nose at the stench of booze. "Justin Geoffrey. Come on, join me in the pub. I'm celebrating my sudden demise."

"Your what?"

"My happy extinction!" The artist did not protest as the odd man dragged him down the sidewalk planks and into an establishment. The talking in the room silenced as all eyes peered at the two gentlemen, and Richard noticed that some few pairs of eyes were of an uncanny silver hue. His companion burst out in laughter and saluted the room with a loud unruly shout. "Greetings, fiends and friends! I bring another outsider into your propinquity! And he is intimate with the first-born beast, so treat him well!" The outrageous fellow turned to smile at the artist, and Richard studied the handsome if emaciated face, the curls of dark Byronic hair, eyes of palest gray. The well-formed and sensuous mouth grinned at him and then hailed a woman who arose at one table and motioned that they should join her. Justin playfully placed an arm around Richard's shoulder and bent to speak into his ear. "That girl's a great fuck," he said, winking at his new acquaintance. He then rushed to the table and gave the woman a passionate kiss on the mouth, and picking up someone's half-drained glass of brew he grinned widely at the crowd and shouted:

"I'm told the tale of some sequestered vale
Where shadow weaves and worms itself between
The spaces of dark trees of ancient girth
Deep-rooted in the supernatural sod.
I've stepped between the spaces of dark trees,
My silhouette rooted to secret mud,
And tasted shadow woven of strange stuff
That spills into my mouth and finds my brain
And warps the very marrow of my bone
And freezes ev'ry element of blood
And pumps my heartbeat to a slower pace
Until my pulse is quiet and I pose
As denizen of tomb."

The artist was astounded at the force and musicality of the voice that chanted poetry, a low clear voice that commanded attention and respect. It hadn't been mere performance – Justin Geoffrey had spoken the verse intimately, as if it were something to which his psyche was irrevocably wed. Although the poet had seemed, upon first acquaintance, mildly intoxicated, his face had taken on an air of sobriety as he spoke, as if some portion of his sleepy brain had been suddenly awakened by the magick of the spoken lines. But then the elfin playfulness returned to his eyes and he roared laughter, thumping the drained beer glass onto the surface of the table again and again, and joined in this action by others in the room. Justin motioned for Richard to join them at the table, and then he addressed the onlookers again. "I present Richard Pickman, late of Boston, here to paint the portrait of our first-born beast."

"It's almost finished," Richard said as he sauntered to the table and was offered a chair by the still-standing young woman. They sat together.

"You're staying above the antique shop?"

"Yes – a curious place, that, with a strange assembly of esoteric stuff."

"Leonidas, the owner, is a fine fellow to know," Justin informed him, "with a goodly supply of rare narcotics. Do you imbibe?"

The artist shrugged. "Now and then – but I prefer to depend on dreams and exploration for my art."

"Then you'll find substance here, in this furtive valley, among these children of shadow and lunacy."

"You're drunk, Justin."

"Not drunk enough, my girl," and he smiled as the barkeep brought a fresh round of amber fluid. "Don't forget, I'm celebrating my sudden and spectacular release from mortal clay." He laughed at the confused expression on the artist's face. "I've been confined in an asylum for some time. Simon and William have mastered my escape, which has utterly perplexed and scandalized those in charge of my far-off penitentiary. To discourage outrage, it has been reported that I died while raving about mine delusions. Rather sweet, the entire comedy."

"Simon and – William?"

"William Davis Manly, my fellow poet. No, he's not among us. He rarely leaves his little hut in the woods. You'll not see him." He pointed to the young woman beside Richard. "That's Hannah Blotch, the imagist poet. We've been trying to convince her that that particular movement has been dead for years, but she is insistent."

"I don't belong to any damn movement – and all good poetry is timeless."

"Then are we all immortal," Justin slurred, finishing another glass of beer.

The others looked up as someone entered the establishment, and Richard turned to see Simon advancing toward their table. He was fascinating by the shift of mood and energy in the room: everyone seemed more alert, and perhaps a bit uneasy. This made him smile – he liked sinister energy. The beast stopped at their table and peered at Justin Geoffrey, who regarded Simon with a sloppy smile. "Sit and join us, beast," the poet invited, "and I shall summon poesy in your honor."

"Nay, sirrah. Your verse annoys me; it has such a diversity of voices."

"I have a plethora of devils in my skull, each of singular expression."

"I prefer consistency of voice and vision. But no matter, I have a small surprise for you, in honor of your escape from that Illinois den. Come – follow me." His eyes, shadowed by the brim of his wide hat, seemed to shimmer with a kind of inner glowing.

Richard was surprised to see that everyone else at the table arose before the poet did, and he stayed seated until Justin finally stretched and indolently vacated his chair. Simon stayed where he stood and took his black pipe from its inner pocket, and the tune he played stirred Richard strangely. The tone was very low and soft, a whisper of melody; but it contained a kind of compelling force that made one's soul ache with longing, and the artist lifted himself out of his wooden chair and followed as Simon finally turned away and exited the place.

IV.

(From the Journal of Richard Upton Pickman)

It was strange – I felt as if I had fallen into an eerie dream, of which I was a part and yet none of which I understood. Like the Piper in Robert Browning's poem, Simon lured us with his music, out of the old building (and it looked very old, that pub, and I will have to return to it anon and smell its secrets) and down the hard dirt road; and in my imagination I thrilled at the idea that he was leading our pack to the mountain and would take us to its secret entrance, where we would encounter a realm of unsurpassed wonder. Although I had been in this uncommon valley for but a few days, and had spent most of those days transfixed in working on my portrait of the beast in his small dwelling just outside the main section of Sesqua Town, I felt a growing kinship with its astonishing inhabitants. I relished the idea, after suffering the growing contempt of friends and family in Boston, that I had stumbled upon a society wherein I felt as one. Simon especially delighted me, for he did not conceal in any way his contempt for all humanity, and I was mesmerized by his sinister aura, by the sense of delicious and playful danger that was triggered at all times in his company. Being in this crowd, now, and tramping into the woods of the valley, felt like being in a wondrous dream, a dream that had aspects of vague familiarity and aroused an ache to remember some forgotten knowledge. Simon's music, for example, as it filtered through the air that night, was like nothing I had ever heard – discordant yet mesmerizing, resembling in its jarring sound an aspect of his personality. The woods through which we tramped were very dark, and I could not investigate some of the more peculiar trees which seemed so bizarrely twisted and malformed, and on some few of which I could just make out, in places where dim starlight illuminated bark, disturbing patterns of moss that almost resembled semi-human faces.

The fabulous darkness of the woods was like a shroud of shadow, and I wanted to tighten it around me; and so I was disappointed when we came to an end of the forest and stepped into a rising field, and I wondered at the way Simon's music softened and became still more strange, as if it were coming from some distant portion of the vaulted sky. I stopped to gaze at that sky and its stars, but then Miss Blotch linked her arm with mine and pulled me back into the bunch. I heard Justin Geoffrey utter an odd exclamation as a lean black column some thirty-seven or so inches in height came into view. At the same time a youngish fellow was coming from another part of the field, pulling a dogcart, and I recognized him as being the owner of the curio shop above which I had my room, a young man named Leonidas. He took to dressing in Victorian attire that seemed to suit him, and on this night he wore a black Inverness cloak. His glossy shoulder-length black hair fell from beneath a top hat that was made of beaver fur or some such thing. Coming to a stop, he held one hand to the quarter moon and made to it an esoteric sign, his sunken eyes flashing with keen expectancy. A number of people gathered around the cart and took up the queerest looking instruments I had ever seen. Simon chose a mammoth coiled horn-like thing that looked incredibly heavy, an instrument that reminded me of a shofar blown at Jewish holidays, but it didn't come from any ram of earthly existence. Shutting his eyes and pointing the instrument at the moon, he blew on it and filled the valley with what sounded like the death-throes of a bull.

My attention returned to the drunken poet, who had fallen to his knees before the column and was muttering to himself. I went to kneel beside him and watched as he ran his fingers over the unfathomable symbols or alphabet that had been chiseled into the stone of the black column. The thing itself was newly made, judging from the high polish of its smooth surface – and yet the object exuded an aura of unearthly antiquity. I tilted nearer to Justin to hear what he was mumbling. "It hasn't been defaced like the one in Hungary. See, see – they are all there! Nothing marred or blotted out. Look at it! Gaze and gaze! What a curious chimera it is, with its hint of semi-transparency – as if it were not wholly of terrestrial realm!" He then turned to me and clutched at my hair, pulling my face closer to the black stone. "Gaze on it, Richard, it aches for light of mortal eyes!" His fingers were tightened in my hair to the point of pain – and yet I did not mind the discomfort, for I had been bewitched. Just as earlier I had been captivated by the sight of the white mountain, now I was completely enthralled with this spectre of smooth sable stone. I did not want to look away, and I grumbled when some valley folk lifted me to my feet and dragged me into their clamorous dance; for they moved about me now like fools on drugs, banging metal implements together, or pounding queer drums, while Simon continued to rupture the night with his heinous bellowing horn. It was a din of madness, efficacious in its ability to rupture one emotionally and imaginatively. My eyes played tricks on me as I looked upward, to the moon, and watched that quarter disc become obscured by nebulous clouds that were not clouds at all, but sprites that billowed evilly above us and wound tendrils between the spaces of the stars. And then a darker cloud-like shape began to form in a place high above the octagonal black column, and as it coalesced I thought it took on such an outline of some monstrous malformed amphibian. I felt its shaping of itself upon and beneath my eyes; and when at last the poet, who was staring at the same delusion, stretched his mouth with awful baying, I howled too, like a lunatic, as around us the silver-eyed children of Sesqua Valley continued with their terrible tumult. I returned to kneel once more beside the lonesome poet, and we curled our fingers into each other's hair.

A naked figure came into my view – Hannah Botch, striped of clothing and dancing like a heathen around the column. Leonidas then came into view, naked as well, his body firm and muscular, and in one hand he held a bunch of long fir switches that had been bound together. He clutched the woman's hair as Justin had clutched mine, and then he began to lash her naked back with the switches that he bore; and she screamed with a mixture of ecstasy and pain, and then she escaped him and spun with amazing speed in a dance that caught exactly the crazy rhythm of the surrounding clamor. She spun, and then seemed almost to float toward one figure who, as he stood, bent low and dug his talons into earth. And then the figure rose and spilled particles of soil over the woman as she fell prostrate before him; and I was shocked to see how the beast, now hatless, had transformed himself, so that as he stood erect and the starlight fell on him I could see how his head had altered and reformed, looking now like a huge wolf's head horribly compounded of elements both human and bestial.

And the horror in the sky drifted too, so as to spread its aether flesh over the black column before which the poet and I knelt; and I watched as wisps of its airy substance coiled toward us and touched our brows. And then the scene turned black, as black as the smooth column of stone, and everything faded from me, like a dream.

V.

He awakened to find himself in bed with a prize headache while a naked woman sat on the chair at his desk and studied pages from one of his old sketchpads. She smiled at him as the red light (of sunrise or sunset he knew not) beamed through the window and tinted her green eyes. "Is this you?" She held up the notebook and showed him a page of a self-portrait he had hastily sketched some few years previously. He nodded, and she squinted her lovely eyes as she scrutinized his face. "My, you've altered. You're far more interesting now. Are you a changeling?" She shut the notebook and bent to return it to the pile on the floor.

"I beg your pardon," he groaned as he studied the sway of her ponderous breasts.

"Were you a foundling? A waif left on some childless doorstep?"

He looked into himself. "I've often wondered."

"You're not completely human, that's obvious. There's a – smell – it clings to the texture of your skin and links you to carnage, to that which is decayed. And there's an element in your eyes that separates you from ordinary men. That's probably why Simon brought you to the valley; it's so unlike him to do that with just anyone."

"I had something I knew he would desire – a family heirloom; and he said he wanted his portrait painted. He attended my last show in Boston and was impressed with my work. I've become fascinated, of late, with the art of photography, and I thought some studies of him in that medium would prove exceptionally absorbing; but he would have none of. 'A pox on that neoteric flashing of false light and the flat image it produces,' he bellowed. 'Give me *real* art, produced of pigment and sweat of brow – or none at all.'"

She laughed. "Yes, that's him exactly. So you just packed up and departed with him?"

"I saw no reason not to. I was in need of a violent change. What was your name?"

Smiling, she rose and joined him in bed. "Hannah."

"Oh, yes – the imagist poet."

"Among other things," she answered as she ran a hand over his furry chest. "You do like girls, don't you?"

"I don't like anyone. 'Richard Upton Pickman is an enemy to humanity.' That's from a review of my last exhibit. It's true enough." He could smell her now, and bent to kiss one breast.

"What excites you?"

"The victorious past – the human past, as it can be sensed in New England, and its present-day survival in this unimaginative era. I like its smell, and its darkness; I relish its secrets and the dangers those secrets cloak. I love the madness out of time that, when sensed by the modern brain, can lead to lunacy and fear."

"And yet the work of yours that I've seen, in those notebook sketchings and on some of the few canvases you've brought with you, are all portraits. You're obsessed with your own alteration, and with its linkage to another colony." Pushing off the bed, she went to a corner where some small canvases were stacked against a wall, and she took up one of them and held it to him. "You also love graveyards."

"I'm fond of that particular burying ground, in the North End of Boston. It's the place I miss intensely. Are there any ancient graveyards here?"

"We have the Hungry Place, where outsiders are dumped."

"That sounds ominous. Take me to it." He glanced out the window and saw that the red light had been replaced with twilight. Rising, he joined the woman in dressing, and then followed as she led the way outdoors. "What's your story?" he asked, inhaling the scented wind that brushed them.

"Grew up in a pious family in Montana. Became a rebel and moved to New York, fell in with various Bohemian cliques and began to write poetry. Journeyed to England with a boyfriend and got involved in a Golden Dawn group, which led to darker practice. Met Simon and was lured to the valley, where I've been ever since. It's an excellent place in which to dwell, as you'll discover."

"It's friendly, certainly – but I've had my fill of the society of men."

"It's friendly only to a few. You don't need to be social at all. You could live as a total hermit, like William Davis Manly."

"Ah, the mystery man that Justin mentioned last night." They came to a low stone wall, and looking over it the artist saw a field of tombstones. "Here we are. What did you call it, the Hungry Place? Why is that?"

"You'll find out." He climbed over the wall easily and waited for her, but she did not seem anxious to join him on cemetery sod.

"What's the matter? Here, take my hand." He reached for her, and she finally clasped his hand and climbed over the wall, then walked beside him as he led the way and examined a row of markers. "This is strange – a lot of these don't have dates, just a first name."

"They are the graves of outsiders, people who have been lured here or found this valley by accident and were too entranced to escape. This is where I'll be buried – someday."

"So is there a section for the valley's special clan?"

"Excuse me?"

"The freaks with silver eyes."

"Only outsiders are buried here. The children of the valley . . ."

"Yes?"

"They return to shadow. Sorry, I can't explain it further; I don't really understand what it means. There's a place in the forest that they return to, never to be seen again. It doesn't happen often, they tend to stick around forever, most of them."

"A singular habitat, Sesqua Town."

"Hell yes. Oh, here's Leonard's grave. He was a chum. We practiced some rare art together."

"Art?"

"Oh, not your kind. Magick. You'll find that Sesqua Valley is a fountainhead of supernatural wonder, as we saw last night."

"That already seems a dream." He frowned, bent his ear as if trying to perceive some sound, and then fell to his knees so as to smooth the soil with his large hands and tough nails. "Do you feel that?"

Hannah frowned and scanned the barren sod. "It is the beating of his hideous heart." She gazed at the man as if expecting him to recognize the words, and frowned when he did not. "A portion of Sesqua's psyche sleeps beneath this place – a very diseased portion of the valley's heart. It warps the ground and infiltrates the human mind. The longer you linger, the more it insinuates itself into your little brain and warps. It's the reason we cannot linger long upon this ground." She glanced at the moon with worry in her eyes as from place deep beneath them a subtle and muted pounding sounded.

Richard dug his hands deeper into earth, and shoved his snout into the displaced soil. "I can taste the corruption of flesh beneath the ground – the appetizing afterward of death. God, I love it."

She knelt next to him and pulled his hands out of their shallow holes. "It's grown late and we should go." But then something in her eyes seemed to alter, and she bent to push one hand into the hole that Richard had produced. Picking up a handful of silt, she brought the stuff to her nostrils and drank its rank bouquet; and then, lifting her hand above the artist's head, she let the stuff sift through her fingers, onto him.

He gazed at her with savage eyes and bent to sniff her throat and bite her ear. "I can hear the blood coursing through your veins – that liquid rush. But too soon its flow is stopped, and flesh cools and becomes dry and rotted. And then the feast begins." His thick tongue explored her throat as her own mouth found his ear, onto which she clasped her teeth. Richard's panting orifice slid downward as his hands separated the opening of her blouse. His mouth tightened around one nipple, and she moaned. His strong teeth pierced her flesh, and she could feel the velvet trickle of blood slide to her belly. Her laughter, when it rose into the aether, was demented.

"Hannah." They both looked up to study the person who stood near them.

"Simon," the artist rasped as he looked upon the fellow.

"Hello, William," the woman corrected. Pushing Richard from her, she rose and took the fellow's hand. He buttoned up her blouse and bent to kiss her eyes, then motioned to the gate, to which she walked and through which she parted, singing to the moon.

Richard steadied himself on his knees and gaped at the fellow whom he had mistaken for the beast – but this gentleman looked younger than Simon Williams, and his hair was darker. His face, however, was almost identical to Simon's. The piercing eyes of that face would not let go of Richard's own. "Follow me," commanded the mellow voice, and Richard rose so as to follow the man out of the Hungry Place. Once out, the mysterious fellow began to whistle a haunting tune, and the sound sank into Richard's ears and calmed his confusion.

And then the artist espied the shapes that were outlined by starlight, the beasts that beat their wings and floated above them in the fragrant air. There were two of them, and they seemed attracted to the gentleman's musical sound. Like shadows in a dream, they drifted to the ground before William Davis Manly. They took each of his hands and placed them at the place where mouths should have been – but faceless creatures owned no mouths. And then one creature bent to Richard and ran its talons across his wide dark visage, and he felt that these things were vaguely familiar. Where had he encountered them, within what realm of fancy?

"They remember you from your dreaming," Manly said. "They would have you follow them, through the other forest and into the dream-land."

"The dream-land."

"There's a place where the Strange Dark One stands in effigy, within a ring of stones that ape his courtiers. It is there that the woodland of Sesqua Valley touches the forest of dreams, when the stars are right. It is from that region that the Crawling Chaos leaks into this pale mortality and warps its denizens with worry. And from that dimension of dream these gaunts have sallied, to the enchantment of my calling, and they would escort you homeward, to she who awaits your freedom from the bondage of mortal clay, from the husk of flesh and its streaming blood. Shall I lead you there, this moment?"

Richard bit into his mouth and tugged at his hair. Why was everything encountered in this valley so extremely insane? "Not yet – not yet. I need to finish Simon's portrait."

"Ever the dedicated artist. That impresses me. Go then, and finalize your task. Then you will be led into the other realm, and never more exist within the hateful world of men." The weird being began to whistle once again, and the night-gaunts stretched their wings and vanished into the gulf of night. Richard watched their flight, and then he turned for more conversation with Sesqua's eccentric hermit; but he was now alone, beneath the bit of moon and blanket of stars.

VI.

(From the Dreaming of Richard Upton Pickman)

I returned to Simon's small house so as to finish his portrait, and was surprised to find that he was not alone. Justin Geoffrey sat on the floor before the hearth puffing on some kind of weed that smelled quite vile. It was not cannabis, nor any substance with which I was familiar; and it was obviously having some kind of effect, for the poet's eyes were almost as pale as Simon's. He peered at me and began to laugh in a low voice.

"You continue to alter," he choked, coughing.

"What?"

"Your face – by god, you look more like one of the valley's

shadow-kindred than ever! And your eyes have turned a darker shade of emerald."

"You have altered as well," spoke Richard. "The quality of your eyes isn't what it was."

"Nope. I am to be initiated unto the fold, adopted by the valley and its kind.

And I will see the world with brand new eyes
And listen to the wind with keener sense,
And taste the sweetened wind that will arise
To wash me of mortality's pretense.
And I will share the essence of the Beast,
And dwell within pure shadow-land anon
As I consume a supernatural feast
Beneath the curved peaks of antique Khroyd'hon."

Simon curled his lips with satanic pleasure. "You shall both of you be altered – and set free," the beast responded.

"Was that why you lured him to this place, Simon? You never do so unless for some specific reason. Is Richard to become one with Sesqua's supernatural essence?"

"No. His destination lies beyond the woodland of reality. William saw it in a dream."

The poet spat into the fire. "I thought your kind was incapable of dreaming."

"It is *I* who never dream. Such a dangerous practice. I have learned to enter mortal dreaming, and debauch it. I reshape the elements of nightmare so that they do my bidding. But I never enter that rare realm myself, nor shall I ever. William, however, is a fervent dreamer, of mystic ability, there in his sequestered lair within a vague pocket of woodland wild. It was he who saw this artist in cloudy vision and told me where I would locate him."

"I met William last night."

"Indeed? That is rare. My brother rarely deigns to shew himself to mortal kind."

"He does resemble you." I forgot about my canvas and went near to the beast, before whom I knelt so that I could minutely study his face and its odd combination of wolf and frog semblance. As I bent to touch his visage his aroma sailed to me more forcibly, a sweet and cloying fragrance such as lingered on the valley air. I bent nearer to him and breathed the texture his face. "Your eyes..."

Tilting to me, the beast kissed my brow. "Yes," he whispered, "they are the one element that will not camouflage within your mortal clime. The rest we can adopt, if we wish, to simulate your form; but our eyes stay as they are in realm of mist and shadow. They are like the stone with which Selta is composed, for it too is incapable of concealing its fantastic element of otherwhere – you can see it in the specks of outlandish color that swim within its rock, those same flecks that float within mine ghostly orbs. I refuse to conceal my nature in the outside world of puny men – let them know me as I am. Let them tremble at my bestial potency. Now, get thee to thy little stool and complete thy task. I admire your ability, and I want this thing completed before you are called by Crawling Chaos."

"What the devil do you mean?"

"Did William explain nothing? Or could you simply not comprehend him? Did the gaunts not suggest your inescapable fate?"

"Those midnight fiends? I've seen them before, when dreaming of my mother."

"Enough. To work."

I went to my stool and sat, took up my implements and began to paint. "That was quite an exhibition in the field."

Justin began to cackle. "It wasn't quite correct. It was too material, Simon. The spectre in Hungary is an historical ghost of a thing that lives no more. The Black Stone has soaked its psychic energy, that is all. Thus, to sleep near that shaft on Midsummer Night is to nourish the energy of that which is dead-yet-dreaming, and so one pays the price of lunacy. I knew better than to sleep there at night. I didn't mean to nap at all – but the thing has its diabolic influence. I care nothing for the loss of reason – the thing inspired my finest book. I confess I ache to look on it again and dream the rare dream."

"One day, Geoffrey, I shall have a replica constructed where now that pigmy imitation stands – a duplication that will have in its assembly shards from the original, shards that were the result of stupid men trying to destroy the Black Stone of Xuthltan. And when the erection of my duplication is realized, we shall build bonfires for the children of men to leap over, and we shall summon the ghost of fabulous darkness and let it sup upon your sanity as we glorify its namelessness."

"It's a deal," the poet muttered, shaking his head enthusiastically. I bent to my canvas and worked until the day was dead, and when the portrait was completed Simon danced in delight at the power of my art. It was quite good, my replication of the beast. I had put much of my own soul into the work, and in one of the shadows that writhe around the daemon I painted a subtle semblance of myself – a smoky presence. When I left the house, Simon was playing his flute, softly, over the poet who slumbered on the floor.

All of this chatter about the Black Stone influenced where I would wander, and I found the woodland way that took me to the meadow, where I found Hannah Blotch petting the black column and singing to the wind. "I can't linger," I told her as she clutched at my pants leg. "I need to locate the place where some strange dark effigy stands before a forest of dreaming."

She shot up to her feet. "The place where the archway stands?"

"You know it?"

"I know its location. It's one of the places forbidden to the children of mist and shadow. It's like the Hungry Place – its effect on them is too alarming and so they stay away. Come on."

Taking my hand, she led the way through another portion of woodland shadow. The trees grew so close together that no light could pierce the place from above, and I relished the absolute darkness through which we scampered. I stopped just once, to study the growth of fungoid moss that adhered to the thick trunk of one patriarchal tree; and I shuddered as the patch of substance, which so resembled a human face, parted its orifice and breathed upon me. Hannah laughed at my reaction, pulled me to her and kissed my eyes, and then she dragged me away. At last we came to a clearing, and I moaned as I looked upon the statue within its ring of stone. I knelt just outside those stones and saw that they resembled small amorphous creatures of diseased delusion, imps that pressed pipes to malformed mouths. Miss Blotch knelt beside me and sighed to the statue in a monstrous language that sickened my soul by its vulgarity of sound. She took my hand, and together we crawled to the icon of the Strange Dark One. My companion rose upon her knees and kissed the statue's obsidian

palm, and then she laughed and, rising, waltzed to the place where
stood an archway composed of weathered red stone.

"Do you know the Elder Sign?" Her voice was a shriek that
sounded like a gale of madness. Reaching down, she picked up a piece
of wood and stabbed it into her palm, then held the bloodstained
member to the sky and shouted more of the monstrous language as
her fingers worked with signaling. I gazed in wonder as the trees just
beyond the archway began to alter, to melt and reform as another
forest composed of stranger elements of shadow. And in that shade I
saw one opaque outline that was a sentient copy of the effigy before
which I knelt. Hannah, seeing the figure, shuddered and wailed, then
floated through the aged archway toward the peril that awaited her. I
shivered as I watched the seven iridescent spheres that formed above
the daemon and the girl, those unearthly seven suns that churned with
cosmic radiance that formed as threads of pseudo-lightning, a light
show of dancing electricity that shot between each sphere. I watched,
as the Strange Dark One caught that play of fire and washed it into the
flesh of Hannah Blotch – her flesh that darkened and crumbled as ash.
I rose and walked to the stone archway, as the eidolon of dread lifted
its facelessness. Something in the smooth blank blackness that should
have contained a countenance seemed to smile at me, mockingly, and
then the spectre melted into the gloom of that other forest and its
assembly of dark mute trees. I heard the tempest that lashed those
trees, an alien storm that fell onto the pile of ash that had once been a
living woman's flesh. I saw that ash rise in coils and assemble as
conscious outline that formed itself into one with whom I had been
intimate – a phantom that kissed my soul with ecstasy and awe. She
held out her dark mutated hands and called my name. The forest was
now completely altered, no longer a place of Sesqua Valley, but of
some otherwhere, and I recognized it as a realm that I had known in
deepest dreaming. I saw the dwarfish imps that peeped between the
spaces of dark mute trees, as above those trees the faceless gaunts
pirouetted in a violet sky, their wide membranous wings outspread. I
saw the seven suns that rose above outlandish peaks whereon the
other gods fumbled in their ancient repose. And I saw she who had
been transformed, her naked skin dark and rubbery, her broad hands
ending in talons designed for digging in cemetery sod, her ghastly

mouth wide and smiling as she mewed my name. I stepped through the archway of ancient stone and loped toward the woods of dream-land, to where my dam awaited me, and fell into her chilly hold.

Host of Haunted Air

Empty you heart of its mortal dream.
The winds awaken...

-William Butler Yeats

I.

I sat at my shop counter, inhaling the heady scent of olden books, my thoughts drifting and transforming into nebulous dream, when the bell sounded at the door. Chilly evening wind moved the brittle pages of the book that lay before me. A figure entered and quietly shut the door. I took in the male attire, clothes that hung askew on so lithe a feminine frame. I smiled at the green carnation in its buttonhole, at the tall black hat that was shiny with age. Beneath the hat's rim dark eyes peered from a wan and worried face.

"Have you see Jonathan since his return from Thailand?"

"No," I answered, closing the book before me. "I've been rather preoccupied with a new shipment. But I expect to see him at your Black and Red party, which is..."

"Three weeks away." She sighed and leaned against a tall and sturdy shelf, looked at her black silk gloves as if she couldn't decide whether to remove them or not. Again, the deep sigh. "Perhaps I'm being foolish." The pause was pregnant with implication.

"Do tell me everything," I coaxed.

"That's just it. I don't know what's up with him. He's been distant, mentally preoccupied. Usually when he comes home from some far-off place he's excited to tell me of his adventures. Now all he does is sit in his pagoda and whistle to himself."

"Hmm. You don't think he's heading for another breakdown or any such thing?"

"I don't know, that seems unlikely. There's something secretive about the way he's acting. That's what really bugs me, I hate being left out. Jonathan's been my intimate companion since father's death, you know. We have a bond. In the past, when something's troubled him, he would always confide in me. I've tried bullying him, you know how he enjoys a bit of brutality; but when I castigate and question he just dismisses me as though I were a clueless child. It's pissing me off. I know he likes his little secrets, his naughty little pleasures or whatever."

"Perhaps he's caught the clap. There is, so I believe, an internationally famous bordello in Bangkok. Or is it Saigon?"

"A case of the clap wouldn't induce him to spend the night in his stupid so-called pagoda." Inquisitively, I arched a brow. "Yeah, I got up to go pee at three in the morning and saw him from my window. He was sitting in the cold wind and rocking back and forth. When I called to him he totally ignored me. Fucking weird."

"Indeed, most curious. And what is it you want from me?"

"Talk to him."

"Well, of course…"

"Tonight."

"But, my dear!" Helplessly, I held up my hands in a gesture to indicate how frightfully busy I was, as I sat there doing nothing.

"Please, Henry. There's no one else. He listens to you."

"But, my dear, *listen* to that brutal wind. Surely this can wait." But I saw from her expression that it could not. With melodramatic sigh I heaved off my stool, wrapped myself in heavy coat and escorted her to her car. The house in which they lived, in a well-to-do lakeside residence, was almost a mansion. This had always been their home. After the death of their father, the two siblings had made few changes inside the house, comfortable with the furnishings they had known since childhood. Their personal lives, however, altered absolutely. Alisha often held gala gatherings for her enclave of bohemian mutants. Jonathan began his series of journeys across the globe, often sending me fabulous old books from far-off lands.

I watched the nighted lake as we drove along the boulevard, until as last we came to the graveled driveway that took us to a high metal fence. Alisha pressed a gizmo and the gate began to move. Their property was so densely populated with towering firs and evergreens that it always had an air of seclusion, despite the constant traffic on the nearby lakeside road. The trees grew so close together that even on the brightest days the house stood in lush shadow.

The gate closed behind us as she stopped the car. "He's in his pagoda," she said, as if dismissing both her brother and myself. Haughtily, I stepped out of the car and slammed its door behind me. The wind was chill and so I pulled my coat's collar tightly around my neck. A line of swaying Japanese lanterns dimly lit the stone path that led across the lawn to the structure that Jonathan called his pagoda, although it but faintly resembled anything found in the Far East. It was like an open garden pavilion with roofing in Oriental fashion. Inside could be found a gigantic Buddhist bell, a fake waterfall and an amazing assortment of wind chimes. The young man sat on a mat, his legs crossed in what I took to be one of his yoga positions. It made my old knees ache to look at him. His long brown hair was tied in a ponytail. He wore sandals, khaki cut-offs, and some kind of fleece vest. With eyes closed he could not see me as I examined his handsome profile, the lean face with prominent cheekbones and goatee. Even in the dim lighting from the single lantern beneath which he sat I could tell that he was darkly tanned, perhaps from his time in Thailand, to which he had journeyed with some Hindu theist. He looked so remarkably composed that I began to question his sister's histrionics.

Chill evening wind died a little; the music of the wind chimes softened. "Henry." I crinkled my brow in confusion. He had not moved, nor had his eyes opened. How then...? "I can smell you on the wind. You reek of dust and old books. I suppose that Ally has asked you to talk to me."

I spoke as I strolled to him. "Yes, but also to ask my aesthetic advice regarding décor for the upcoming festivities. But she does seem just a tad bit worried. Are you behaving beastly? In one of your tiresome moods?"

"No. I've merely been preoccupied. She simply wants something to fret about, you know how she is. She wants this party to be a fabulous success."

"Ah, that might be it. And you're being childish because she is so focused on her party that she is ignoring you. You're both such spoiled children, clamoring for center stage."

"You're stupid if that's what you think."

"Pardon my benightedness," came my bitchy reply. The wind buffeted us once more, and at the sound of clanging I looked at the swaying chimes and saw the new addition. But exactly what it was I could not ascertain. At first I thought it some freakish papier-mâché head, but as I drew nearer it looked more like a metal object encrusted with blue dusting of granulated steel. It had a kind of face; where the mouth would have been it wore an oval aperture the size of a small egg. Two lesser holes suggested nostrils. Where a face would have had eyes were two shallow indentions, but these were solid, sans orifices. Above these, on what might have been a forehead, was a grouping of tiny pea-sized holes that numbered seven.

"Mmm, something new."

"Oh. Yes." I sensed a change in his decorum, a sudden frigidity. Turning, I peered at him and saw his face filled with wonder, and in the eyes a tinge of terror. He moved his eyes from the thing of metal and noticed my expression. Hurriedly, a torrent of language spilled from his babbling mouth. "I found it in Bangkok, in a curious little shop. There was a main room filled with the most god-awful American junk. But I found this little alcove near the back, dimly lit and cluttered, just the kind of place where I find those old books that so delight you. And there it was, sitting among a disarray of jumble. I thought it was some kind of weird wind chime, so of course I bought it."

"It looks rather unearthly."

How nervously he cackled. "Indeed."

I touched a hand to its rough surface. How frightfully cold it was. With what an unnatural – nay – a *disquieting* texture it had been composed. Frowning, I took my hand away. My fingers almost burned with chilliness; and with something else, some kind of nasty residue that adhered to my numbing flesh. Disgusted, I rubbed my fingers on my trousers. A noise caught my attention. I leaned closer to – the thing – and fancied that I could hear wind moving through it. Stepping around so to examine the back of it, I was startled to see a solid surface with no opening of any kind. But surely that was the mitigating wind that moaned through it, its sound somehow distorted as it sailed through the thing's apertures.

I looked at the length of chain from which it hanged, from a small yet sturdy hook that had been soldered to its top. Moving, I faced its front. Had the night grown nippier, or was it creepiness that tickled my flesh? I sensed the night wind fade away. The chimes around us stopped their insistent movement. All was dead quiet, except for the faint suggestion of sound that issued from the thing before me -- and Jonathan's faint whistling. I looked at him, with his wide eyes oddly glazed and his moving mouth askew. The mingling of sounds seemed seductive, so beguiling that I leaned closer to the egg-shaped opening so as to hear the better. Yes, I yearned to listen, to press against the course uncanny surface and listen to the air that moved within. Perhaps if I were to press my lips together I too could whistle in imitation of its eerie sound. Perhaps if I touched my mouth to the small opening...

A hand tightened at my shoulder and pulled me away. I shouted in protest, and then saw Jonathan's panicky eyes peering into my own. Something in their troubled expression filled me with fear, and together we fled the haunted place.

II.

I fidgeted in a chair before a fire. Jonathan had taken me to the expansive library room, and after having prepared coffee for me had fixed himself a large martini. I held the cup of scalding liquid tightly in my hand, grateful for its warmth. Now and then I glanced into the fireplace; but I quickly looked away, troubled at the things I saw, or thought I saw, within the flames.

"Now. Jonathan. Explain to me, please, that which has just occurred."

"What?"

"No, do not suddenly play ignorant. You will explain to me this – thing – in your pagoda and its unnatural effect. What it is?"

He paced the floor, refusing to sit; nor would he look at me. "It's what I told you it is." He saw that I was growing agitated and angry. "It's obviously some weird kind of wind devise."

"It's 'obviously' like nothing we've either of us seen before."

Sighing in frustration, he finally sat. "Okay. Yes, it's unusual, and has its eerie effect." I snorted. "I can't explain it. But, Henry, we are susceptible to such effects because of our senses. Sounds, music, can either soothe or disturb us. Look at what happened when Stravinsky premiered *Le Sacre du Printemps*. People went mad, the performance ended in riot. Or take thunderstorms, of which you are so partial. Some people run and hide, while you rush to the nearest window. We are creatures of our senses, rational or not."

I pouted. "You are trying to placate me with calm tone and soothing language. Yet not twenty minutes ago you *hurled* me from that place with terror flashing in your troubled eyes."

"I thought you were going to kiss the damn thing! You had the oddest expression on your face. Of course I dragged you away, I haven't cleaned it yet. God knows where it's been or by what it has been pawed."

"I am not placated."

"Then fuck you. " Jonathan rose and fixed himself another drink. My pouting deepened when I saw that he would offer me no refill of the bad coffee. Muttering obscenities of my own, I placed the cup on a nearby table. "Look," he continued, "I agree that the thing is kind of creepy – stop snorting! The thing is, I like it, whatever the hell it is, and that's the beginning and end of it. Tut all you like. I found it, I liked it, I bought it." He glared at me with defiant eyes.

"Very well. I wish to speak with Alisha."

"She'll be asleep. It's late. You're tired yourself." I wanted to protest, but my yawns spoke otherwise. "Come on, I'll drive you home. Just let me change into some trousers."

"I'll meet you out at the car," I told him, yawning again. Wearily, I rose and went outside, into wind and darkness. I felt distraught, emotionally drained. I did not understand the events that had just passed, but was suddenly too tired to care. Turning my eyes to the wretched pagoda, I saw its single lantern move in wind. I saw the shadows that swayed on the figure that stood beneath it, facing – the thing. Standing very close. I was momentarily distracted when Jonathan came out of the house, slamming the door behind him. The echo of sound reverberated in the aether. When again I looked to the pagoda, it was vacant of human occupant.

III.

Days passed. I had received a wee note from Alisha, apologizing for the "nonsense" of the previous evening and formally inviting me to her ball. I decided to go as the Red Death. An obvious choice, perhaps. My other idea was Little Red Riding Hood, but there are limits even to my perversity. A flowing crimson robe would conceal my girth and look superb. As time passed, I oft reflected on that strange evening. I dwelt on that thing of encrusted blue metal, and saw it in deepest dreaming. Betimes I caught myself listening attentively to the wind, fancying that it hummed a variation of the weird tune that Jonathan had whistled when I had been captivated by – the thing. I knew not what else to call it, and so it was – the thing. Yet the more I pondered on it, the more mysterious a thing it seemed, something alien and bad. Yet beguiling. I burned to look at it once more, to touch it – perhaps to kiss it.

At last the festive night arrived. I taxied to the mansion and was let in through the gate by an awaiting knight. I wandered below high swaying trees, moved through oscillating shadow and playful wind. My eyes followed the line of Japanese lanterns to the pagoda, and I hesitantly stepped toward the structure. Its hanging chimes danced in the air. The sphere of blue metal was nowhere to be seen.

"Henry." Jonathan stood a few yards away, holding to me his long pale hands. I walked to him, took his hand, allowed myself to be escorted into the house.

"Your strange new thing…"

"Missing," he said, shrugging. That was all; he offered no explanation or conjecture. I felt a peculiar sadness, and a kind of panic that I did my best to conceal. We stood in the hallway, examining each other. He looked resplendent in black tux and cloak. The only red was in the contact lenses placed over his eyes. He grinned at my ghoulish makeup, showing two sharp fangs. Together, we entered the ballroom.

And an alternative world, a diabolic one. The crowd was much as I had expected, beautiful boys in scarlet gowns, masculine women in coat and tails. Somber music was piped in the room from unseen speakers, and bowls of incense filled the place with fragrance. From one darkened corner I espied Alisha, who smiled and slightly bowed. She was magnificent and original as the Lamanite king, Amalickiah. My eyes feasted on her indigenous beauty as I stepped to her. With masculine courtesy she offered me her hand to kiss.

The room was like some fantastic phantasm. The walls had been elegantly covered with drapery of ebony and maroon velvet. Cushions of similar shade littered the floor, upon which groups of youngsters sexually explored each other. I watched as from one of these groupings a young figure arose. Despite the wild orange wig I recognized him as a lad who oft frequented my bookshop and who had a fascination for the yellow decadence of the late Victorian age. I was charmed to see him dressed after Beardsley's splendid work of ink and color wash, "The Slippers of Cinderella." He took from his apron one of the disintegrating roses that had been pinned thereon, and this he offered me with benedictional bow. "To the Great Lord Thanatos, the only god before whom I grovel," he declaimed. I took his flower, cupped my hand below his chin and pulled him to me. His breath reeked of champagne. Bending to him, I kissed him hard.

"Well," Jonathan muttered, "how swiftly you get into the swing of things. Come, I've a special concoction just for you." He led me to a serving station at which a manservant poured dark liquid from a sparkling silver coffee pot. I took the delicate cup proffered me and brought it to my nostrils, breathing in the brandy with which the coffee had been laced. Normally I had no stomach for liqueurs, but on this night I refused to be a prude. I sipped, and smooth delicious nectar spilled into my mouth, warming my face.

Time passed. After a number of coffees I fell upon a cushion and smiled idiotically at the surrounding sexual frolic. Finally, Alisha clapped her hands and the music ceased.

"Mesdames et Messieurs, the Dance of the Seven Veils."

True decadence crept into the room. What they were, I could not fathom. I had read somewhere of a race of cannibalistic semi-human dwarves who dwelled in some plateau somewhere in Central Asia. These creatures could have hailed from such a tribe. The twisted features of the hateful faces had a sobering effect. They profoundly repulsed. I watched as the ones who carried flute instruments sat in semi-circle and placed their pipes to misshapen mouths. The room was filled with discordant piping. A diminutive figure wound in flowing veils danced into the room. Its gyrations moved in rhythm to the esoteric music, and one by one the veils gradually fell from its stunted torso. I saw the small dry breasts and the twin genitalia both male and female.

People began to hoot and applaud as Alisha slowly danced toward the nude monstrosity, holding a silver platter on upturned palms. A sheet of black silk covered the object that tilted on the platter. Ally knelt before the bestial gnome and I watched as the creature removed with knobby fingers the covering of silk. I had, of course, read Wilde's play, and thus I expected to see a grisly replica of the head of Iokanaan. Instead, I beheld a sphere of blue metal.

Shrieking pierced the room. Rushing wildly to his sister, Jonathan took the sphere, clutched it to his heaving breast and dashed madly from the place, into night. Trembling, I arose from my cushion. Figures surged around me, shouting cries of drunken confusion. Blindly, I ran from the scene, seeking silence and solitude. Instinct led me to the lonesome library, with its soothing and familiar world of books. Ah, the wondrous scent of ancient paper bound in leather. And there was the large leather sofa, where on more than one occasion I had slept when allowed to spend late nights poring over Jonathan's volumes. Moaning with aching pleasure, I staggered to the sofa and fell upon it. Happily, I succumbed to dreamless slumber.

A delicate hand smoothed my hair and pulled me out of sleep. Alisha sat beside me on the edge of the sofa. "What time is it?" I asked.

"Almost dawn. Everyone's gone."

Swiftly, I sat up. "Jonathan!" She shrugged. "What on earth do you mean by that absurd motion?"

"He's vanished." Her face was pale, but her eyes very dry.

"Then we must find him! He has – that thing!"

"It can wait. You need more rest." Her voice was soothing, calming, hypnotic. I tried to protest, but her hand – so smooth and white – pressed against my lips. "Hush." Groaning in suitable demurral, I allowed myself to sink again into the depths of delicious somnolence. Alisha hummed a haunting melody, one that would have disturbed me were I not so fatigued.

When again I awakened, I was alone. I felt rested, yet worried. Something, some unwelcome sensation, had shaken me from slumber. And then I heard it, from outside, the sound of whistling. And my blood froze, for the dissonant din was identical to the horrid music that had been played by that gang of goblins on their evil flutes, played to the sphere of blue metal. I pushed out of the sofa, stumbled over my long scarlet robe and hurried to the library door. All was hushed. The dull light of early dawn was skulking through the high windows. Fearfully, I found my way outside. The air was cold and very still. I saw the figure who knelt within the pagoda. I went to her. How strangely she smiled as I approached. I wanted to speak to her, but some unspeakable horror kept me numb and silent. I bent my knees and joined her on the ground. Leaning toward me, she pressed her cool mouth to mine. She puckered and exhaled. Both she and Jonathan were skilled at whistling, with a tone that was sharp and forceful.

"Please," I begged her. "Stop."

She did not heed me, but rather gazed into the early light, her eyes suddenly rapt with wonder. The chimes above us began to sway. I turned. The thing stood just outside the pagoda. I took in the dark torn garments. It had lost its splendid cloak. The long dark hair was too caked with blood to stream in the growing gale; some of it was crudely wound around the metal hook that pushed out of the top of the human head. One crimson contact lens still covered a wide dead eyeball. The open mouth was imbued with gore, and from that orifice there came a low unearthly sound of moaning air. Here and there the flesh of the face was torn, showing the blue metal beneath the skin, the damnable blue metal that had somehow conjoined with once-living tissue.

Alisha's lips pressed against my ear. "It hungers for our hot mortal air." Like a thing possessed she rose. I was too deadened with terror to try and stop her as she walked to that which had once been her brother. My blood was icy sludge, my limbs heavy with immeasurable horror. I watched as the young woman pressed her mouth to the mutation's outrageous visage. How oddly her frail body jerked; what ghastly noise rattled from her pretty mouth. At last she fell before me. I wept to see that she was a lifeless shell, her once-lovely mouth bruised and blue.

The thing towered above me, not moving; yet somehow I felt it beckon me. I heard from beneath the dead face a noise of ravenous air, air not of this earth. Sobbing, I shut my eyes, trying to exorcise the nightmare before me. On my eyelids I could see the tendril shadows of swaying chimes, and my ears took in the music of wood on wood, metal on metal, glass on glass. Most horrible of all, I could feel the hunger of the thing that summoned.

I opened mine eyes. I stretched my sensitive limbs and rose. I lurched to that shell of dilapidated humanity that had once been my friend, but was now my awful, my inescapable doom.

A Vestige of Mirth

The thing before me shook with vulgar motion as it vomited hilarity. Its absurd mop of tangled hair fell before wide blank eyes, and its torso jiggled so violently that I expected the dummy to slip from its chair. Backing away from the large cabinet of wood and glass which housed the mammoth toy, I smiled; and then all motion ceased, the thing stood dead still. My nickel's worth of time was up.

The round man behind the counter grinned with impious glee and softly chuckled. "My granddaddy made it 'fore I was born, when he built this store in '78. It was a modern wonder back then, pulled in huge crowds. Great for business. Course, back then it worked with pumps. My daddy rigged it so it'd work with 'lectricity. Somethin' else, ain't it?"

"It is indeed, Walter," I agreed, glancing at the nickel slot and fighting the temptation to watch once more. The old man gazed at me with wide eyes set deep within a rubbery face, and then he pushed buttons on an antiquated cash register and totaled my bill. Opening my wallet, I gave him money. He eyed the food and drink that I had purchased as I dropped them into my backpack.

"Gonna take in some sights, are ya?"

"Yep, I want to hike some country. Thought I'd follow the railroad tracks along the riverside and head for those distant hills."

"You want to watch out for rattlers, Joe. It's crawling with snakes up there. Ain't tryin' to put you off or nuthin', but jest be careful."

"Will do, Walter, thanks." Turning to the door, I moseyed outside, squinting at pale autumn sunlight. A cool breeze was blowing from the river. Pulling on my backpack, I strolled toward the water until I came upon rusty railroad tracks. In the few days that I had been in this small town, I hadn't heard or seen a train go by, and so I assumed that the line was not in use. Happily, I hopped onto one of the rails, balancing as I walked with arms outstretched. I had been quite adept at this when a kid, but adulthood had dulled my talent. Slipping onto dirt and rocks, I bent to pick up a smooth round stone, which I tossed over the river's surface. I walked for an about an hour, following the tracks until they turned away from the river and headed into an area of rocky hillside. Cautiously, I scanned the ground and nearest hills for snakes, but saw no living thing. The air grew still, which I found odd; surely the breeze I had experienced would sail between these hills of red rock. But nothing stirred, and I slowly sauntered through the hushed surroundings, until at last the hills were behind me and I looked out onto a great expanse of flat open land.

The curious object stood still in the distance. At first I thought that it was a derailed freight car of odd design; but as I approached it I saw that the metal wheels were not intended for railroad tracks. The wooden surface had once been painted yellow, but now a faint remnant of color covered the splintered wood. Spectral letters formed a name that was too faded to make out, large though the letters had been. This was obviously some kind of carnival car, from a sideshow that had long ceased to exist. As I neared a doorless entryway, an unpleasant meaty odor assailed my nostrils, and I wondered if an animal had somehow become trapped inside and was rotting in death. Gingerly, I leaned into the doorway and peered into a world of curious horrors. Shelves had been built into the walls, and on one long shelf I saw a series of mannequin heads covered with deteriorating rubber masks, the decaying pieces peeled and bent like the brittle leaves of a dead plant. On another shelf I saw a series of fantastic bestial forms, creatures of ludicrous combinations that looked like the work of some insane artist who had a talent for creating macabre fakes. How strangely realistic they looked, these concoctions; how brightly their black eyes beamed, reflecting the sunlight that filtered through the great holes in the compartment's roof.

I heard no sound of movement, saw no sign of feasting vermin. Placing my hands flat on the wooden floor, I heaved myself into the car. My clumsy feet stumbled as I rose to a standing position, and my arms grabbed the nearest object in order to prevent my fall. The object before me was an old kinetoscope, such as I had seen in curio museums. I knew that this neglected and timeworn gadget couldn't possibly work, especially as there was no source of electricity; and yet I couldn't resist rummaging through my pants pocket for loose change. Feeling foolish, I dropped a nickel into the coin slot and gasped as the machine began to whir and creak. Hesitantly, I pressed my forehead against the padded leather of the peephole. I saw nothing but blackness, and supposed that the machine's source of inner illumination had long expired. Yet, as I continued to watch, lulled by the mechanical purring, I detected a suggestion of moving shadow in the blackness into which I peered. Something fumbled and flowed, expanded closer to the viewing glass. It seemed, this crimson-tainted blackness, to bubble, as if hungry to leak into my eyes. Frantically, I backed away and blinked at sunbeams.

The antique gizmo shuddered and died. My panic subsided. Again, I became aware of a rancid stench, and when I looked behind me its source was discovered. There, on a long low table, was a grouping of large glass jars. The pulpy objects inside them gently swirled in thick ruddy liquid. As if on cue, one of the soft spongy things paused in circulating and bumped against its glass prison. I thought at first that it was a variation of the weird rubber masks, albeit one of more lifelike rendition. I didn't like its wide liquid eyes, and I felt peculiarly nonplussed by its idiotic smile. As I gazed at the wretched thing, its carrion smell seemed to increase, filling my mouth with bile. Hurriedly, I rushed to the doorway and jumped onto solid ground, heaving spit and air.

Beneath my retching I heard another sound, a curious kind of music. It brought to mind a damaged jack-in-the-box from my poverty-stricken childhood. The tune that played as I gently turned the crank was distorted, seemingly incomplete. The mindless music that fumbled from the other side of the car was of a similar nature. Beguiled, I sought the source of sound, feeling again the sense of fear I knew as a child that turned a little crank and waited for the macabre jester to pop out of its box. What I suddenly beheld was no less clownish. I could not fathom what the figure was supposed to be. At first glance it suggested a sad-faced hobo clown I had once delighted in while attending a circus; and although the creature before me now was dressed in hobo fashion, it certainly was not melancholy. Rather, this darkly dressed buffoon joyfully pranced to the warped music, clapping large white hands as it shook with jocundity.

The thing that squatted near to the farceur was inexplicable. It might have been a kind of deformed monkey, or a dwarf costumed very badly as a beast. Just as peculiar was the instrument that was cradled at its crotch, a kind of makeshift hurdy-gurdy from which the staccato noised issued. I did not like the way the creature obscenely turned the crank that produced sound, nor the way its partner wagged in time to the outlandish rumpus. Foolishly, the clown waved at me, then bent to a wooden wash basket into which it dipped its large pale hands. I stared as those hands emerged, now defiled with dripping gore. Happily, the funny gentleman tossed the globes of filth into the air, juggling them as crimson drops splashed all around. The creature watched expectantly as the balls of blood floated for one moment and then fell onto his gleeful face. The music stopped as the jester turned his eyes to me. The wet red fluid entirely covered his face, and I helplessly witnessed as the thick lips of that face pursed and blew. A bubble of blood began to expand from the wide inhuman mouth.

I stood transfixed as the liquid ball separated from the monstrous maw and rolled in the air toward me. The vagabond jiggled with joy, and his familiar jerked spasmodically as it ferociously turned its crank. A cacophony of awful pandemonium assailed my ears as the bubble of blood collided with my face. All was instantly silenced. I blinked but could not see clearly. A ghastly scarlet fog swirled all around me. Slowly, I began to make out nebulous forms. I saw a buffoonish figure hopping toward me, while scuttling at its feet was a shaggy figure that held a large and empty glass jar. Huge discolored hands reached for my face. Instantly, I was sightless. But, oh, I could *feel*. My legs seemed to slip from me, and the heavy pack no longer pressed against my back. Hot liquid baptized my flesh as flabby fingers worked that fabric into a kind of sphere. Then the hands were gone, but not the warm red mist. I floated in a carnal pond, and pushing forward I bumped into a wall of glass. Through that glass, darkly, I saw the jolly man lift his bestial companion to the shelf of rotting masks. The wee creature clasped one of the shredding heads and pulled the floppy rubber over its pate. Winking, the masked one pointed a talon at me. I watched as the wicked member began to circulate, and as I watched I too began to gyrate. Dimly, as I turned, I beheld my squashy crony in the jar next to my own. Something in the sardonic curl of his too soft lips proved intoxicating, and stupidly I smiled.

The caravan began to thump with rhythm. I could hear no sound, but I saw the twin grotesqueries flailing playfully about the room. The dwarfish thing leaped into its master's arms, and together they approached my prison. The shattered visage of the masked one peered into my jar. Perversely, its jaws parted and a twin-tipped tongue snaked forth and touched the glass. How it was possible that I could feel the pressure of that purple porous appendage against my flesh I do not know; but the touch of it so titillated that, god help me, I laughed until I split.

About the Author

W. H. Pugmire has been writing professionally since 1985. An obsessed H. P. Lovecraft fanatic, his work is most often in the Cthulhu Mythos vein. His many books, published and forthcoming, include THE TANGLED MUSE (Centipede Press), SOME UNKNOWN GULF OF NIGHT (Arcane Wisdom Press), THE STRANGE DARK ONE – TALES OF NYARLATHOTEP (Miskatonic River Press) and UNCOMMON PLACES (Hippocampus Press). He is currently working on two collaborative books: one with Maryanne K. Snyder, in which all tales will be inspired by the weird fiction of Clark Ashton Smith; and with Jeffrey Thomas, a series of tales concerning the sinister New England artist, Enoch Coffin – forthcoming from Dark Regions Press.